Janwani
जनवाणी

I0691038

green growth

GUIDE TO A MODEL GREEN CITY

Arun Firodia

GREEN GROWTH
Guide to A Model Green City
by Arun Firodia

Copyright © Arun Firodia

First Edition: January 2017

ISBN 978-93-85665-63-9

JANWANI
505, MCCIA Trade Tower
Senapati Bapat Road
Pune-411006 (India)
www.janwani.org

Published by:
Vishwakarma Publications
283, Budhwar Peth, Near City Post, Pune
411002.Phone No: (020) 20261157 / 24448989
Email: info@vpindia.co.in
Website: www.vpindia.co.in

Design and Layout:
Falguni Gokhale and Rasika Pawar
DESIGN DIRECTIONS PVT. LTD.
Ph: 020-25653902
www.designdirections.net

वंदे मातरम् ।
सुजलां सुफलां मलयज-शीतलाम्
सस्य-श्यामलां

Mother, I bow to thee!
Rich with thy hurrying streams,
Bright with the orchard gleams,
Cool with thy wind of delight,
Dark fields waving...

Message
Dr. A. P. J. Abdul Kalam
Former President of India
Bharat Ratna

I am happy to receive the copy of the book 'Green Growth' by Shri. Arun Firodia which is published by Janwani. Indeed, this is a very relevant topic not just for the nation but also for the world.

As we all know, human activities are contributing more than 32 billion tonnes of Carbon dioxide every year in the atmosphere which is already creating alarming symptoms of global warming and climate change. With increasing population and disposable incomes, such trends will only rise unless we take action to address them. Out of the total CO_2 generated, around half is absorbed in natural sinks of ocean and soil. This means that around 12 Gigatons of additional CO_2 is released into the atmosphere. Scientific calculations shows that one part per million (1 ppm) roughly corresponds to about 7.8 billion tonnes of CO_2. This means that we are adding about 2 parts per million of Carbon dioxide every year. Such imbalalnce have been more significant since the industrial revolution. Analysis shows that the CO_2 concentration has risen from the pre-industrial figure of around 280 parts per million in 1750 to about 384 ppm in 2007.

We know that energy supply is the highest contributor and contributes around 26% of the overall emissions, largely due to the burning of fossil fuels to generate electricity. Industries generate more than 19% of the global emissions and deforestation contributes another 17%. Agriculture too is responsible for about 14% of the global GHG emissions. The entire transport sector put together is responsible for about 13% of the global emissions. The rest of the emission comes from the residential and commercial sectors, waste and wastewaters.

The impact of global warming is already being felt across multiple environmental aspects and throughout the world. Meteorological data shows that there has been a significant upward trend in the average temperature in all the continents across the globe. In the past two centuries, the rise in the temperature has been almost 1^0C on land and more than 0.5^0C in the oceans reflecting an overall rise of 0.8^0C.

Message
Dr. A. P. J. Abdul Kalam
Former President of India
Bharat Ratna

In fact, since 1970, most of the regions and countries of the world have witnessed temperature rise of varying intensities.

Today we have a clear challenge before us which is that of building a sustainable environment. This can be done by conservation of ecology and mitigation of existing and future climate changes. To achieve this, we have to find confluence of technology, management, social science and policy. This will need a combination of actions including green energy, green living, biofuels, solar powered homes and afforestation – even at micro-level tree plantations.

I came across in the chapter on domestic consumption where the author has analysed the prospect of rooftop solar PV systems. He has calculated a required total investment of about ₹ 80,000 per kilowatt of installed power. Further, taking Maharashtra as a sample case, he has determined that after 10 years of pay-off period for a loan – the electricity will cost ZERO for the next 15 years. In the same section, he has also pointed out that how Direct Current Solar Powered Home could lead to a further saving of 30% or higher.

I was pleasantly surprised to read how Firodiaji has calculated that if we all switched from electric bulb to CFLs, the payback period will be less than 200 days, lead to saving of 54% in the domestic energy consumption overall.

Towards the end of the book, Firodiaji has highlighted how all of us can together realize clean green planet earth. He has envisioned a roadmap to make city of Pune completely carbon neutral, as a result of the action of citizens, industries, transportation and government sector. He has calculated that the city of Pune can produce over 4.8 billion units of electricity every year using rooftop solar giving a turnover of over ₹ 1400 crores for the city. Coupled with this, he has planned for a solar powered transportation sector and efficient domestic fuel planning. He has also laid out a detailed plan for usage

Message
Dr. A. P. J. Abdul Kalam
Former President of India
Bharat Ratna

of biomass to generate power using processes like briquetting and napier grass. Finally, the author has asked, can we make earth a paradise? Yes, I agree – we can do it.

Planet earth is our home and it is our duty and responsibility to protect it, not just for us but also for generations to come. We must nurture the planet and keep it livable.

My best wishes to Shri. Firodiaji in his mission to bring about Green Growth for a cleaner earth and a happy nation.

Dr. A. P. J. Abdul Kalam
New Delhi

Message
Prof. M. S. Swaminathan
Father of Green Revolution in India
Padma Vibhushan

I have gone through 'Green Growth' with great interest. The model that has been provided in the book for a 'green' city could be the basis for the 'smart city' programme of the Modi government.

Mr. Firodia's suggestion that we should have a shift from macro to micro approach if we are to make development sustainable is a good one. I also agree with him that we should say goodbye to a high carbon lifestyle. The other areas he has discussed like solar power for domestic uses, rainwater harvesting, and green transport are all very relevant and possible. Finally he has given an excellent blueprint for carbon neutral Pune using solar, wind and biomass. Rainwater harvesting should also be included. In fact it should become mandatory.

His final question, "Can we make earth a paradise?" is a good one since it emphasizes the importance of public participation and public action. Ultimately, we have to go to the Gandhian pathway of fostering harmony with nature and with each other.

'Green Growth' is a timely and important contribution, since 2015 marks the beginning of the UN decade for Sustainable Development. I congratulate Mr. Firodia for providing a blueprint for human survival and sustained happiness.

Prof. M. S. Swaminathan
Chennai

Foreword
Prof. C. N. R. Rao
F.R.S.
Bharat Ratna

The phenomenon of climate change is no more an idea, but a reality. People around the world are afcing the severity of extreme weather events and their frequency is increasing. In order to mitigate the impact of climate change we need to act now.

Each new problem offers new opportunities. In the case of climate change. The opportunity lies in ensuring sustainable development. Areas of renewable energy and energy management have the potential to employ thousands of engineers and scientists, but there is need for modifying the technologies according to India needs. Particularly in fields such as bio-power and hydrogen. Abundant availability of sunlight can be harnessed to split water into hydrogen and oxygen by artificial photosynthesis. Discovery of affordable, eco-friendly and easy method of production and storage of hydrogen can be a panacea to solve our burgeoning energy demand if we switch over to hydrogen economy.

For this purpose, the manpower of the nation has to be focused on research to solve the urgent social needs like energy, environment and water. India has to work harder than others because of our heavy dependence on monsoon and to safeguard us from the crisis of climate change.

Sustainable development is not just matter of technological development. It has to be accepted by society. For this purpose, we should not only focus on technology but use it with an environment-friendly approach that would satisfy society.

In the light of Paris talks and the new legally binding universal agreement on climate change, 2015 is a very crucial year. In this context publication of 'Green Growth' is timely. It attempts to inculcate values of sustainability in society. I congratulate Mr. Firodia for his timely contribution, since this book highlights ability of India and other developing nations to aim for sustainable urban development. Rather than merely insisting on technology transfer in the climate change agreement, this book prefers, 'Yes we can do it, on our own'.

I thank Mr. Arun Firodia, for analysis of the broad range of topics and compiling them in an easy-to-understand format. It bridges the gap between serous research and social needs. Often overlooked by researchers.

I hope that each city in India will draft its own climate adaptation plan, in order to make the earth a paradise, again.

Prof. C. N. R. Rao
Bangalore

Foreword

Dr. R. Chidambaram
Principal Scientific Advisor to Govt. of India
Padma Vibhushan

Energy is the driver of growth, and for the Human Development Index in India to come to the levels achieved in the already-developed countries, the per capita electricity consumption has to grow manifold. This objective has to be harmonized with the climate change threat, which requires the share of low-carbon electricity supply from sources like renewables and nuclear to increase. One of the main themes of this book is to provide solutions which mitigate the threat of global warming and reduce the carbon footprint.

More generally, the book is an expression of anguish by the author at growing global problems like global warming, and at urban problems like water shortage, water and air pollution, etc., followed by possible solutions to these problems.

Every city receives electricity from large power systems located outside, but can reduce its energy requirements from such systems by using solar and wind power, generated within the city. The author has tried to give a road-map for making Pune 'carbon-neutral', through wide-spread use of roof-top solar installations, use of high-efficiency electric appliances, green architecture and efficient transport systems.

The discussions on transport, shifting away from high-carbon personal vehicles to low-carbon public vehicles and introduction of electric and hybrid vehicles, municipal solid waste treatment and sewage treatment are excellent.   As the author says, these require not only advanced technologies, but also behavioural changes.

The book is eminently readable, explaining the relevant issues in simple comprehensible language, without sacrificing accuracy. I enjoyed reading it very much. I must congratulate the author Shri. Arun Firodia, who comes out as a rational optimist in this book 'Green Growth', which inter alia charts out his dream of making Pune 'a model green city'.

Dr. R. Chidambaram
New Delhi

Preface
Roadmap to Sustainability

The human race faces many problems. Hunger, terrorism, racism, poor education, income inequality, gender inequality, superstition, lack of civil rights ... the list is daunting. Planet Earth also faces an equally long list of problems. Global warming, water shortage, floods, water pollution, air pollution, typhoons, deforestation, extinction of species, new viral diseases like swine flu ... again the list is long and unending.

It is time for the human race to find solutions to these man made problems. Indeed, time is running out and we have only a few decades to set our house in order.

This book is an attempt to find solutions to the problem of Global Warming.

It is now known that global warming is due to emission of Greenhouse Gases. The problem is serious and daunting, but the good news is that it is possible to address it and overcome it. This book attempts to show how we can do it.

First we set a comparatively easy goal at a 'Micro' level and then try to find out ways to achieve it.

The easy 'Micro' goal the book has attempted to achieve is : Can we, in the year 2020, reduce Greenhouse Gas emissions in Pune City to the level of year 2010? Pune is a city in India with a population above 3 million. While reducing emission levels it has to be ensured that the recent rising tempo in standard of living is maintained too. What steps are needed to be taken by individuals and authorities to achieve this comparatively easy goal? What would be the costs to achieve this goal? Is it possible that savings in energy usage more than offset these costs? Fortunately, the answer is yes.

Next, we aim higher. Can we make Pune City 'Carbon Neutral'? That would be ultimate in sustainability. Do the technologies exist for achieving this ambitious goal? Are the technologies simple enough to implement? Once again, can we save a tidy sum for ourselves while making Pune Carbon Neutral? Would you believe that the answer is yes. This book lists various steps to achieve this goal. And the obvious corollary is 'If Pune can be Carbon Neutral, every Indian city can also aspire to be Carbon Neutral'. How exactly to do that ?

The methodology adopted is 'Realize', 'Reduce' and 'Replace'.

Realize:
The first step of any project is 'assessment of situation'. In this book we have referred to TERI's 'Carbon Inventory Of Pune City-2012' report as the baseline. That gives us the emissions in various sectors such as domestic consumption, transport, institutional consumption and municipal solid waste.

Reduce:
The second step is to see if energy consumption could be reduced in each of these sectors while maintaining a rising standard of living. There are some 'low hanging fruits' where investment required would be minimal whereas the emission reduction would be substantial? We should identify such low cost solutions and start working on them right away.
It is a generally accepted notion that rich countries emit more CO_2 than poor countries. While this is true we should also consider that poor countries would become middle income countries and aspire to reach the standard of living of presently rich countries. When the poor countries

become rich would they emit less or more? Would they learn how to become 'carbon efficient' during the decades on their way up the economic ladder? It is pertinent to note here that India emits about 1.350 Tonnes of CO_2 for per \$1000 of GDP while Japan emits a mere 0.262 Tonnes per \$1000 of GDP. This indicates that we consume more energy than others for obtaining a given amount of income and this energy is generated from carbon intensive sources like coal. This would have to change. Obviously we need to use energy more efficiently.

Let us take the example of the transport sector. Rail transport consumes 30% less energy than road transport. If we complete dedicated railway freight corridors expeditiously that would save considerable amount of energy. Similar is the case with water navigation. It is even more energy efficient, thanks to the buoyancy of water. However the total cargo moved (in tonne kilometers) by the inland waterways on India is just 0.1% of the total traffic, compared to 21% in USA. Another important area to focus is the groundwater table. Agriculture pumpsets consume 19% of total electricity in India. Lower the ground water level, higher is the energy consumption for pumping. Groundwater level has fallen precipitously in the past few decades due to excessive pumping. This can be reversed by watershed development i.e. storing rainwater in small checkdams or wells in the vicinity of the village itself. Gujarat has demonstrated this very effectively. Other states too have embarked on similar projects on a war footing.

Replace:
Not only do we need to save energy, it is important to generate the energy from renewable 'non-carbon' sources. That needs investment in sources like solar , hydroelectric, wind and others. That obviously requires heavy funding by the Government. In order to encourage a shift from carbon-

intensive energy to green energy many nations are considering imposing Carbon Tax. Some have even imposed it. Concept of 'carbon tax' is not new to India. We already have tax on coal at ₹ 50 per tonne, which is too meager to fund investment in energy efficiency projects and renewable energy sector. The Carbon Tax needs to be raised substantially and the large revenue generated from Carbon Tax should be used for investment in green energy.

Can entire India aim for Carbon Neutrality? Abundantly endowed with renewable sources of energy such as solar, wind, hydroelectric and biomass, India can be Carbon Neutral too. If a densely populated nation like India can do it, then the entire world can also become Carbon Neutral. That would usher a veritable paradise on earth.

Of course Planet Earth faces many other serious problems like water shortage, floods, water pollution, air pollution, typhoons, deforestation, extinction of species, new viral diseases like swine flu, etc. mentioned above. This book is a practical guide to achieve the task of overcoming just one of them - 'Global Warming' - that too at zero net cost.

The forewords by the most distinguished scientists of India, Prof. C. N. R. Rao and Dr. R. Chidambaram, have added great depth to the book. The messages by Former President of India, Dr. A. P. J. Abdul Kalam and by father of India's Green Revolution, Prof. M. S . Swaminathan have taken the book to great heights. I cannot find words to express my gratitude to them.

If the book arouses interest in the readers and the authorities about the problem of global warming and if they decide to take concrete steps to mitigate it, the effort will be well worth it.

Acknowledgements

This book contains serious research. Young scientists Chinmaya Kulkarni and Vishwesh Pavnaskar did the entire research while working for Janwani, an NGO working to make Pune the most livable city in India. My sincere thanks are due to them. I spent hundreds of hours working with them and enjoyed every minute of it. Ravi Pandit and Vishal Jain, trustees of Janwani and Dr. Kulkarni, Director of Janwani made valuable suggestions and contributions. So did Santosh Gondhalekar in the field of Biomass. Rajesh Upasani provided many illustrations . The entire team of Janwani pitched in with suggestions, insights, facts and figures; sincere thanks are due to them. Falguni Gokhale, the eminent designer, did a masterful job of designing this book . The task was difficult as the book contained many tables and graphs and looked like a Ph.D. thesis, but she converted it to an eminently readable book. If the book serves its purpose, they get the credit. All the errors of omissions and commissions are mine.

Contents

What is Climate Change?

Why Is It Important?

Climate Change - is a very simple term - it implies a change in climate. 'Global Warming' is yet another simple term that is frequently used. These two terms together lead us to think that climate change is occurring on a global scale, and, as a result, climate is warming up, little by little.

We have all heard comments from grandparents that Pune residents never needed fans in 'those' days. Does that mean that installing a fan could be our simple solution to the warming climate? Shall we just ignore the brouhaha of global warming and get on with our lives with help of a fan? Or, maybe, an air conditioner?

No, the implications of climate change are far more serious. Especially for India.

India is highly dependent on the monsoon, particularly, agriculture. A timely and plentiful monsoon yields bumper production of food grains and vegetables, thereby keeping food prices under check. Even more important is self sufficiency in food. It is a matter of strategic importance and cannot be compromised at any cost.

Agriculture employs 51.1% of India's labour force[i] and their livelihood is dependent on the monsoon. If the monsoon is below par, millions of our people suffer heavily even to the point of starvation.

The monsoon gets affected by climate change and therefore we more than any other country in the world, need to take it very seriously.

Monsoon

Monsoon winds are created by the temperature difference between the surface of the Indian Ocean and heated parts of the Asian land mass. If the wind flow over India gets disturbed due to climate change, there could be a catastrophe in store for India in form of famines or drinking water shortages or even desertification. It may be noted that the difference in temperature over the ocean is a mere few degrees. Small temperature changes could change the direction in which the monsoon wind flows. Indeed, studies show climate dramatically affects the quantity and quality of the monsoon.[ii,iii]

Indian crops require an initial heavy downpour after which farmers sow the seeds. After sowing, there is need for a respite from the rainfall otherwise the seeds might just get washed away. After the seeds sprout up, the crop needs alternate sunshine and rainfall days. When the crops have fully grown, there is need for bright sunshine to prevent diseases swamping the crops. Then there is need for a heavy downpour during the 'reverse monsoon' which brings moisture from the Bay of Bengal to the Indian Peninsula. This rainfall helps the second (*Rabi*) crop which is as important as the first (*Kharif*) crop. The point is that the exact timing and amount of rainfall during the growing season are very important. In the event of global warming it is predicted that there would be long periods of dry days followed by long periods of heavy rainfall days.[iv] That would be disastrous to production of established food products, except maybe rice.

Climate change poses further grave threats, like a rise in sea level, hailstorms and typhoons, flooding as observed in UK and Pakistan, heat wave in Russia and increased diseases.

Sea Level Rise

Sea level rise is among the most easily understood effects of climate change. As temperature rises, the glaciers melts, the Arctic snow melts and sea levels rise. Research published in 2010 by the US National Research Council suggests sea levels could rise up to 1.8m[v], which could submerge many densely populated low-lying or reclaimed urban areas like Nariman Point or Mahim in Mumbai, or coastal Netherlands. Sea water would intrude into river deltas and coastal freshwater swamps and marshes[vi]. That would reduce yield of fish. It has already happened in the Mekong delta in Vietnam[vii].

During the 'Ice Age' people could walk, and did walk on foot most of the way from Andaman to Australia. Due to melting of snow the sea levels rose and we got cut off. So sea level rise is not just a figment of imagination of a scientist. It has happened, and that too not very long ago. We have to be mindful of that eventuality.

Glacier Melting and Kedarnath Flood

The Kedarnath flood was not just a flash flood due to heavy rains and cloudburst, but it was a cumulative effect of global warming and environment degradation. Due to climate change glaciers started melting rapidly leading to formation of lakes. One such lake was formed above Kedarnath. In June 2013, heavy rain and a phenomenon called the Glacial

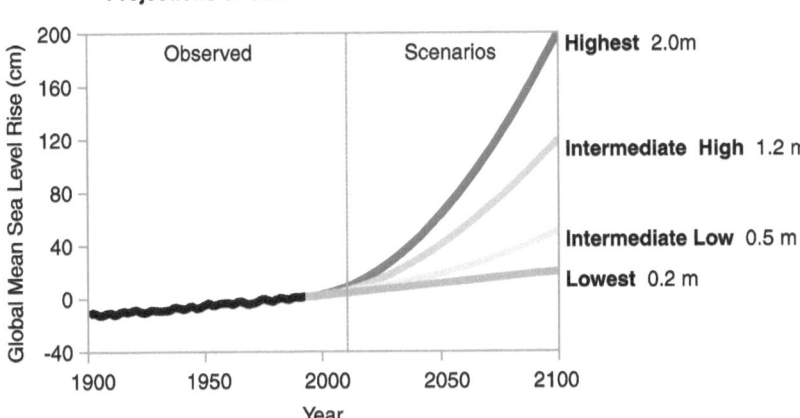

Projections of Global Mean Sea Level Rise[viii]

Lake Outburst Flood (GLOF) happened simultaneously, and washed out Kedarnath. Water flowed into the valley, taking sediment with it, thereby making it deadlier. The phenomenon of glacier outburst is new to the Himalayas. It happened due to global warming which led to melting of glaciers. This means more and more glacial lakes will be formed in the coming times, leading to potential disasters.[ix]

The effects of such floods will not remain limited to the Himalayan region. The Himalayan rivers flow down into northern India. Putting the area under potential risk of heavy floods.

Increased Disease Burden

There are viruses which are prevalent in an equatorial warm climate. The ecosystem there is used to these viruses, so they do not cause much harm. When the climate of the temperate zone warms up due to global warming, these viruses migrate to the new warm climate zones. The ecosystem there is not familiar with these viruses. So they can cause epidemics like Influenza. Senior citizens are particularly vulnerable to influenza as it can lead to pneumonia.

4

When white men entered America they brought with them germs and viruses with which their bodies were familiar and which did not cause them any harm. But the native 'Indians' succumbed, when exposed to these unfamiliar germs and viruses. It is said that more native 'Indians' got killed by coming in contact with the unfamiliar germs and viruses than by the white man's guns !

Since global warming is going to encourage spread of viral diseases, we should seriously worry about it.

Greenhouse Gases

There are gases called 'Greenhouse Gases'. Carbon Dioxide, Methane, Nitrous Oxide, CFCs and HFCs, Sulphur Hexafluoride, Carbon Tetrachloride, and even water vapour are greenhouse gases. These gases act as a blanket around the earth, preventing heat from leaving the earth's atmosphere. In fact, they send the heat back to the earth's surface. This 'blanket effect' is known as the greenhouse effect.

The greenhouse effect is very significant. In its absence the average surface temperature of the earth would be around $-18^{0}C$, instead of the current value of $15^{0}C$. That is, the greenhouse effect has led to an increase in average surface temperature of $33^{0}C!^{x}$ Clearly, the greenhouse effect is extremely important. In its absence, water on the planet would be largely frozen. Life as we know it would be impossible. The present levels of greenhouse gases are optimum for human life and activity. If the levels of greenhouse gases were either much higher or much lower than the present levels, the consequences would be very serious.

5

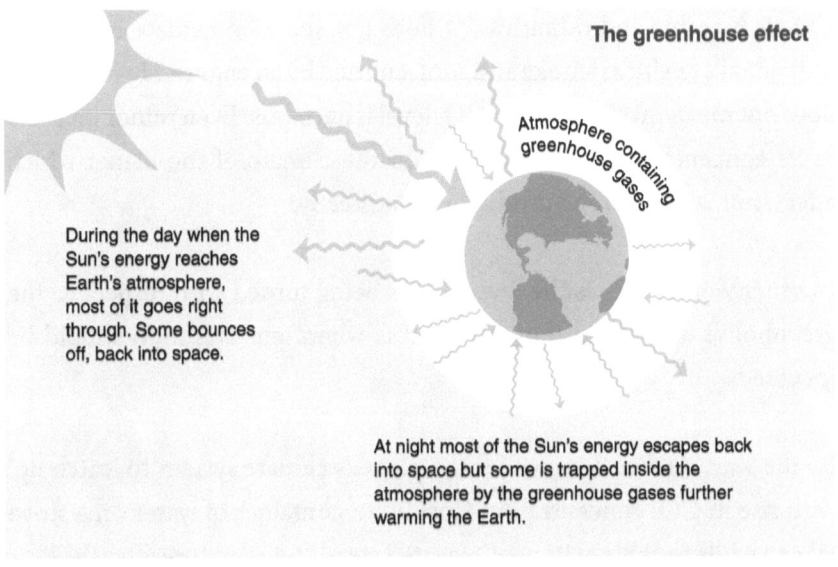

The greenhouse effect

Atmosphere containing greenhouse gases

During the day when the Sun's energy reaches Earth's atmosphere, most of it goes right through. Some bounces off, back into space.

At night most of the Sun's energy escapes back into space but some is trapped inside the atmosphere by the greenhouse gases further warming the Earth.

Source: climatekids.nasa.gov

Carbon Dioxide Is an Important Greenhouse Gas

There are many greenhouse gases in the atmosphere, all of which have a role to play in the greenhouse effect. Why, then, is carbon dioxide (CO_2) the focus of our book, and indeed, of discussions about climate change across the world? Well, because it is an extremely important 'greenhouse gas'.

The industrial revolution in the mid-1800s saw the invention of the steam engine that started the industrial revolution. Next came the plentiful supply of electricity grids and production of automobiles in 19th and 20th century. That accelerated the pace of economic growth. Electricity required burning of coal and automobiles required burning of petrol and diesel oil. Burning of these fossil fuels released CO_2 into the earth's atmosphere.[xi]

6

CO_2 is invisible and odourless. It does not show immediate impact on individual's health as smoke and soot, emitted by an engine. However that does not mean that increase in CO_2 level is harmless. Even minor increase in its concentration has an impact on the climate of the planet which affects human health and productivity indirectly.

In other words, CO_2 is the lever that is being turned with respect to the greenhouse effect, and therefore that is where our attention should be focussed.

By the way, it takes decades for the planet's climate system to 'catch up' with rise in CO_2 concentration (just like a container of water on a stove takes a while to achieve its new, elevated steady temperature after the heat supplied from the burner has been increased); Therefore we should know that the full impact of a rise in CO_2 concentration will continue to be felt only over the next few decades. Even if CO_2 levels stop increasing right now, global warming will go on for decades to come. A frightening scenario indeed.

The current level of CO_2 is 401.88 parts per million (ppm) while before the industrial revolution in the 19th century, global average CO_2 was about 280 ppm. During the last 800,000 years, CO_2 fluctuated between about 180 ppm during Ice Ages and 280 ppm during interglacial warm periods. Today's rate of increase is more than 100 times faster than the increase that occurred when the last Ice Age ended. [xii]

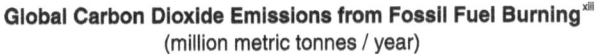

Global Carbon Dioxide Emissions from Fossil Fuel Burning[xiii]
(million metric tonnes / year)

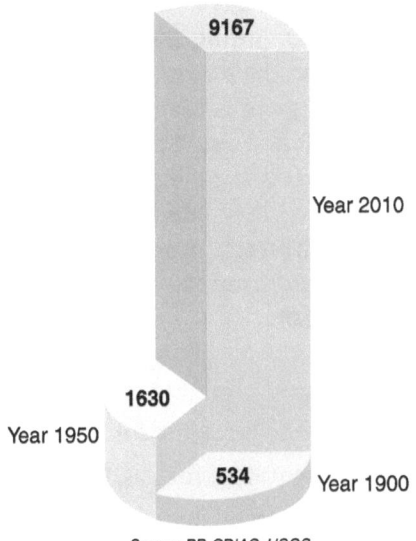

Source: BP, CDIAC, USGS

What is Carbon Footprint?

The term 'Carbon Footprint' refers to greenhouse gas emissions caused by human activities. Different greenhouse gases have different potencies; they also have varying lifetimes, the time span during which they last in the atmosphere. For example, methane is a much more potent greenhouse gas than CO_2. However, it gets oxidized in the atmosphere, and therefore does not last as long as carbon dioxide. The varying potency and lifetimes of

CO_2 has been the driver of climate change throughout the recent past of the earth's geological history. Records going back 800,000 years[xiv] indicate that CO_2 was a major player that ultimately forces earth's climate one way or another.

8

We think that trees absorb CO_2 and if we plant many trees CO_2 levels would come under control. However it may be pointed out that while trees absorb CO_2 during the day, they give out CO_2 during the night. Only when the tree is growing it absorbs more CO_2 during the day than it gives out during the night. If, after the tree is fully grown we cut it and use it as firewood, it would give out all the CO_2 it had stored during the growth phase. However it should be acknowledged that planting trees have many beneficial effects like biodiversity, providing shade and shelter, humidification (and therefore reducing temperature and even inducing creating rainfall), etc.

greenhouse gases are taken into account for the purpose of carbon footprint calculation. The more potent the gas, the larger is its footprint. Similarly, the longer the gas lasts in the atmosphere, the larger is its footprint. For sake of simplicity, the contribution of each gas to warming is declared in terms of its CO_2- equivalent.[xv]

Electricity and petroleum fuel have become the largest contributors to CO_2 emission, and we should study them a little bit deeper.

Electricity and Carbon Footprint

We are familiar with term 'unit of electricity' because our monthly electricity bill is proportional to the units of electricity consumed by us. A unit of electricity is the amount of the electricity consumed by a 60 watt bulb for 16 hours and 40 minutes, or a 1.5 kilowatt water heater for a mere 40 minutes. Each of these actions amounts to consumption of one unit of electricity. And is responsible for emitting 800 grams of CO_2 to the atmosphere!

Electricity seems such a clean form of energy and one may wonder what the connection between electricity and CO_2 is. In India, most of the electricity is produced at thermal power plants by burning coal. Therefore the calculations show that use of one unit of electricity gives rise to emission of 800 grams of CO_2. Electricity generation by hydroelectric and solar photovoltaic plants is, obviously, much cleaner and is preferred from the point of view of CO_2 emission.

Petroleum Fuel and Carbon Footprint

Petroleum consumption and CO_2 relation is easier to understand. A petrol car emits 189 grams of Carbon Dioxide per kilometre whereas a bus emits 763 grams of carbon dioxide per kilometre . Since the bus carries 40 people, then the emission attributed to each person is only around 22 grams per kilometer. In other words, if each of the 40 people in a bus were to use a petrol car, the emissions would be 7,573 grams, or 8.5 times the bus's emissions![xvi]

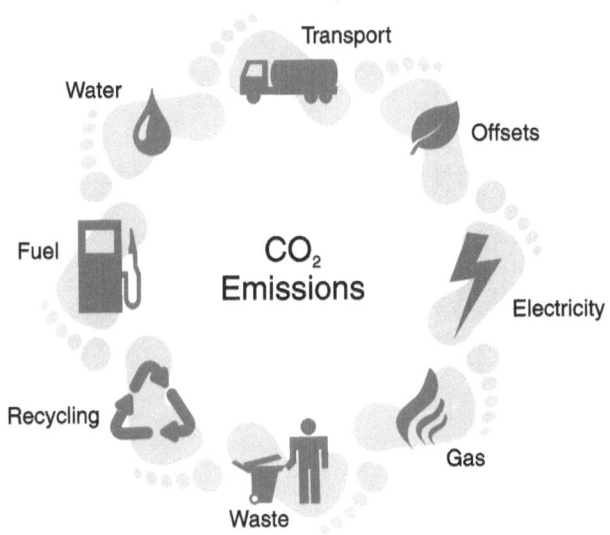

The figure below shows the relative emissions of some modes of transport. An LPG cylinder causes 42,300 grams of carbon dioxide emissions. Assuming that it lasts for 100 meals for a family, cooking one meal for a family would cause 423 grams of carbon dioxide emissions.

If lighting a bulb causes CO_2 emission, if cooking a meal causes CO_2 emission and if going to work causes CO_2 emission, what should an ecology conscious family do? Stop all such 'normal' activities and go back to a caveman's lifestyle?

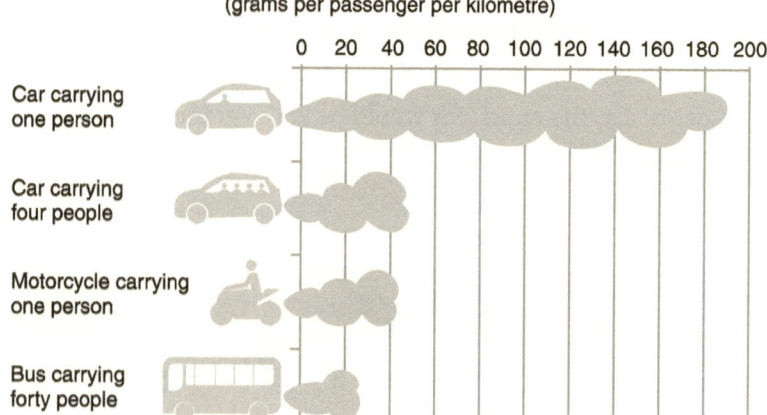

Carbon Dioxide Emissions for Different Modes of Travel
(grams per passenger per kilometre)

Dilemma: Development or Environment?

Energy use is the largest contributor to global warming. 67% of all global greenhouse gas emissions, and 86% of carbon dioxide emissions, are due to energy use in one form or another[xvii]. Therefore reducing energy use seems best way to mitigate greenhouse gas emissions and global warming.

On the other hand, energy is a key driver of all forms of development, and a key necessity for human endeavours. Indeed, the quantity and quality of energy use are often considered to be an important marker of economic and human development.[xviii]

There exists an abundance of empirical evidence to highlight the relationship between energy and different indices of development.

For example, Figure 1 shows the per capita electricity consumption of different countries, plotted against income per capita. Each dot in the figure represents a country. It is evident that there is a strong correlation between electricity consumption and income (which in turn in strongly linked to other indicators of welfare). As electricity consumption goes up, so does the income, and vice versa.

Additionally, Figure 2 shows the relation between total energy consumption per capita and income per capita for India, from 1971 to 2010. Again, a strong positive correlation is evident.

We may conclude that energy is necessary for development. But can we satisfy our energy needs without harming environment? Energy use has this huge impact on carbon dioxide emission and climate. On the other hand it is essential for human welfare. Environment or development is the

Figure 1: Electricity Use v/s Income Per Person Per Year, 2011(log scale)

Source: gapminder.org

Figure 2: Electricity Use v/s Income Per Person

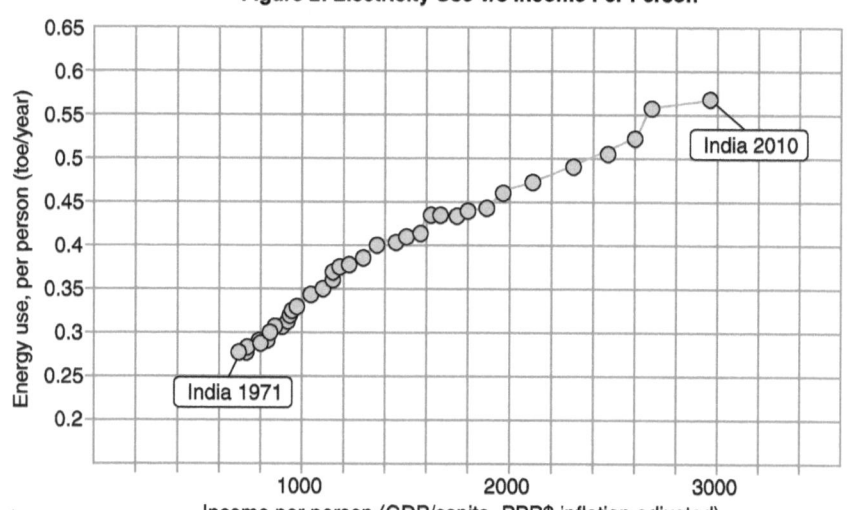

*toe: tonne of oil equivalent

Source: gapminder.org

dilemma before us. Can this dilemma be resolved? Can development and increase in standard of living be achieved while simultaneously achieving reduction in Carbon Footprint?

As our study below shows in reality there is no dilemma and environment and development can take place simultaneously.

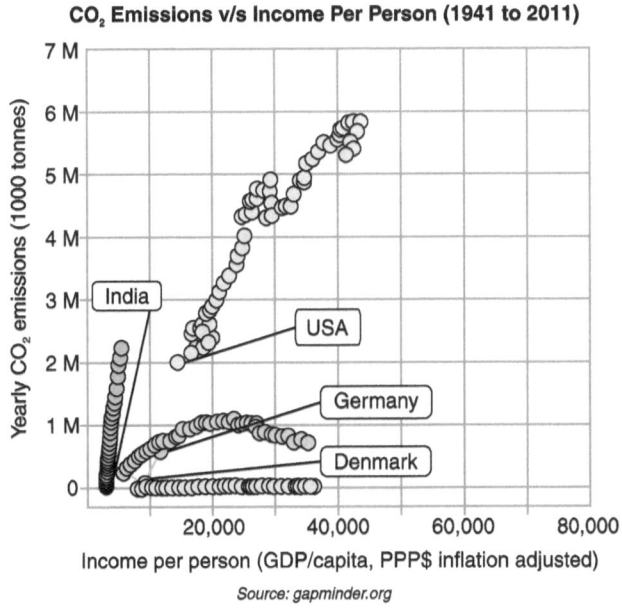

CO_2 Emissions v/s Income Per Person (1941 to 2011)

Source: gapminder.org

Let us study how four countries that have carried out their development and have adopted different 'energy' policies. This graph tracks annual CO_2 emissions by four nations from 1941 till today. United States of America (USA), India, Germany and Denmark. What do we understand from this graph?

Development of USA is done at the cost of the environment. Annual CO_2 emission increases as per capita income increases. This is not in case of Germany and Denmark. Till 1977 - 80 Germany was also progressing at

14

the cost of the environment but after that due to determined efforts and following environment friendly ways it achieved progress and actually decreased annual emissions! The case of Denmark is very interesting. Being rich in the natural resource of wind, Denmark has achieved development without any rise in emissions.

India has progressed just a little but emitted much more. Surely there is need to review our development model and follow the path shown by countries like Germany and Denmark.

'Macro' to 'Micro' Approach of Sustainable Development

A target can be achieved only by proper planning at various levels. In case of environment, Intergovernmental Panel on Climate Change (IPCC) has set targets at the global level. These are enshrined in Kyoto Protocol and 'Agenda 21' published at first earth summit. This is 'Macro' approach. To achieve the 'Macro' target we have to plan at 'Micro' levels. Such plans have to be in line with macro plans but need to be based on local needs. India too has as prepared its macro plan called 'National Action Plan on Climate Change (NAPCC)'.

India's Macro Plan

India's CO_2 emission, in the year 2010 was 1.41 MT per capita. The world average was 4.5 MT per capita. India's Prime Minister made a declaration that her per capita emission will never exceed the average per capita emission level of developed countries. This is laudable considering that China's per capita emission (5.92 MT) now exceeds that of France (5.04 MT).[xix]

We should give up 'carbon intensive' development and adopt 'carbon light' development.

India had further announced in 2009 that it would aim to reduce the emission intensity of its GDP by 20 to 25%, over 2005 levels, by the year 2020. This is a very serious commitment since India's energy intensity is already equal to the world's average! It means that India cannot keep increasing its emission by claiming that its per capita emission is lower than that of developed countries or that its people need more energy to increase their standard of living. It means that India may increase its standard of living but by adopting 'Carbon Light' development policies.

Micro Plan of Pune City
In line with this, we propose a Micro plan for Pune city, in accordance with IPCC and NAPCC's 'macro plans'.

In the following chapters we present a case study of Pune city to show how the carbon footprint, and therefore contribution to climate change, can be reduced significantly. That too while preserving the momentum of development.
Specifically we have covered 3 sectors:
• Domestic Consumption,
• Transport, and
• Institutional Consumption.

In these chapters we will find out:
• Carbon Footprint of each of these 3 sectors in the year 2010.
• Predict what the Carbon Footprint in 2020 will be if we do not take corrective steps ('Business as usual' scenario). But we will not stop there...
• We will suggest ways of going back to 2010 levels. "
• Then we shall see if we can make Pune carbon neutral.
• If the answer is yes, this book can serve as a guide to a model green city, anywhere in the world.

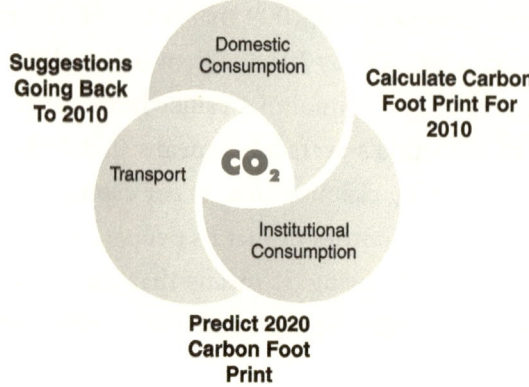

Can we do it?

Yes, we can.

Determined efforts by Pune residents, the Pune Municipal Corporation (PMC), the Maharashtra State Government and the Central Government will help to reduce the carbon footprint.

Working together we should be able to reduce the carbon footprint in 2020 to what it was in 2010. That will also help India achieve its commitment of reducing its energy intensity by 25%.

If we achieve this target, we will be doing service to our planet. We will also derive health benefits for us and our children. Not only that, during the process, we save thousands of crores of Rupees. It is unbelievable but true!

Appendix

[I] As per an economic survey carried out by the Ministry of Finance in 2010

[II] Arathy Menon, Anders Levermann, Jacob Schewe. Enhanced future variability during India's rainy season. Geophysical Research Letters, 2013

[III] Turner & Annamalai (2012); Climate Change and the South Asian Monsoon, Nature Climate Change 2: 587-595

[IV] Allan & Soden, 2008

[V] America's Climate Choices: Panel on Advancing the Science of Climate Change; National Research Council (2010): 'Advancing the Science of Climate Change' pages 243-250

[VI] Cruz et al, 2007

[VII] Halls et al. 2009

[VIII] Parris et al, 2012

[IX] http://www.thethirdpole.net/climate-change-poor-policies-multiply-himalayan-flood-effects

[X] Qiancheng Ma (1998): 'Greenhouse Gases: Refining the Role of Carbon Dioxide' NASA-GISS Science Briefs, accessed at http://www.giss.nasa.gov/research/briefs/ma_01/

[XI] Evidence for this comes from an isotopic observation known as the Suess effect.

[XII] NOAA Media Release 'Carbon Dioxide...Tops 400 ppm' (2013), http://co2now.org/

[XIII] Fossil Fuel Use Pushes Carbon Dioxide Emissions into Dangerous Territory by Emily E. Adams (EPI website)

[XIV] European Project for Ice Coring in Antarctica (EPICA)

[XV] Generally over a 100-year time horizon. Therefore, carbon footprint is usually reported in terms of carbon dioxide equivalent (the 100-year time horizon is often implicit)

[XVI] Assuming car milage as 12 kmpl, 3 kmpl for bus and 50 kmpl for motorcycle.

[XVII] As per 2005 data from the World Resources Institute

[XVIII] White's law states that cultural development itself is driven by a society's ability to harness energy and by its ability to effectively use that energy to do work.

[XIX] Planning Commission Reports

[XX] In this book, we adhere largely to the scope followed by TERI's Carbon Inventory of Pune City (2012). That is, we consider emissions that take place within Pune's geographical boundaries (specifically, emissions associated with petroleum consumption and solid waste management and sewage), and those associated with electricity generation for Pune but not transmission and distribution losses.

Carbon Footprint for Domestic Consumption

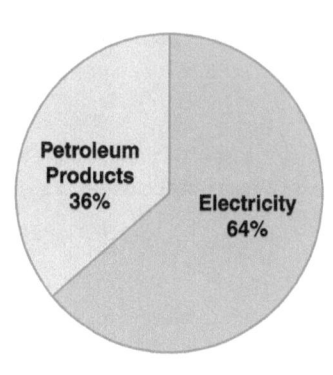

Petroleum Products 36%

Electricity 64%

In the year 2010[i], the domestic sector consumed 1635 million units of electricity[ii] and accounted for 1308 kilotonnes of CO_2 emissions.[iii]

Petroleum Fuel was the other important contributor to CO_2 in the domestic sector. It consumed 151 kilotonnes of LPG and 43 kilotonnes of Kerosene, and accounted for 587 kilotonnes of CO_2 emissions.

In 2010 alone, the domestic sector emitted 1,895 kilotonnes of CO_2 emissions

Due to domestic consumption alone, each resident of Pune was responsible for 608 kg of CO_2 in one year.

This is approximately 10 times the body weight of the *Punekar*.

CO_2 emission due to driving of vehicles, generating waste, etc. is not included in this calculation.

Domestic Consumption

Now let us take a look at the domestic sector. This sector touches our everyday lives. We live, breathe, eat and work in this sector. The emission of carbon dioxide is also highest in this sector. The good news is that, the possibility of savings is also highest in this sector. We will study the following two aspects:

- Carbon Footprints in 2010 and 2020
- Change in our life style, from the 'high carbon' lifestyle to 'low carbon' lifestyle, to go back to CO_2 emission levels of 2010.

As mentioned in the previous chapter, 'Carbon Footprint' is created mainly by energy use. In the domestic sector, we use energy in the form of electricity and petroleum fuel. Electricity is used to light our home/office, to power appliances, to heat water and to do many more things. Petroleum fuel is used in the form of Liquid Petroleum Gas (LPG) mainly for cooking.

Residential as well as low tension commercial consumption are grouped under 'Domestic Consumption'. This is because CO_2 reduction strategies are similar in both.

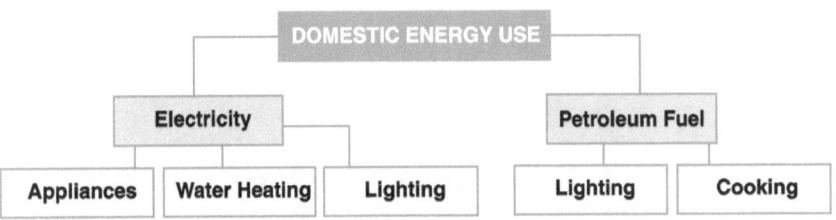

Five years prior to the year 2010, electricity consumption in domestic sector had been growing at 9.65% CAGR (Compounded Annual Growth Rate) and Petroleum Fuel consumption at 5.82% CAGR[iv]. We assume that the same trend will be followed in the future[v] as standard of living of Pune residents will continue to rise.

If the growth in consumption continues at the same rate and if we do not take any corrective actions, in the 'Business as Usual' scenario, the CO_2 emissions in year 2020 will rise steeply. This is illustrated in the following table and graph:

Domestic consumption	CO_2 emission in 2010	CO_2 emissions in 2020 in 'Business As Usual' scenario
Electricity	1,308 kilotonnes	3,007 kilotonnes
Petroleum Fuel	588 kilotonnes	890 kilotonnes
Total	1,895 kilotonnes	3,897 kilotonnes

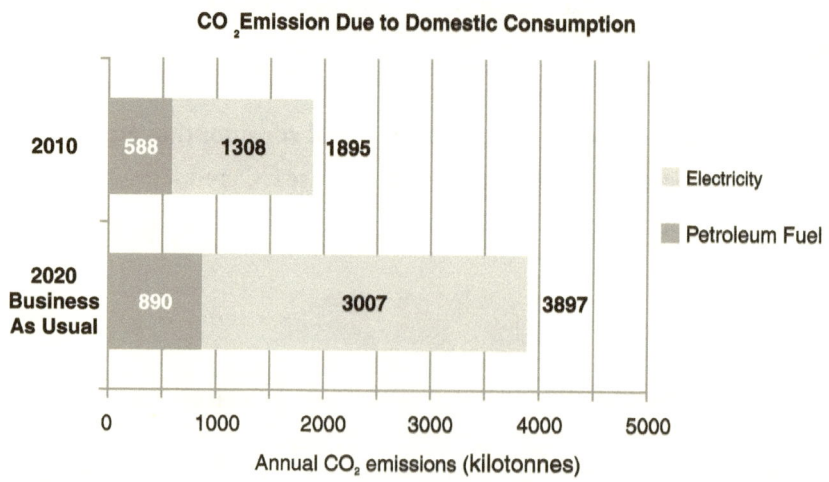

CO$_2$ Emission Due to Domestic Consumption

Obviously we need to take corrective steps. We need to reduce energy consumption while maintaining the growth in standard of living.

Let us further analyse the end use of electricity and petroleum fuel in the sub-sectors of domestic sector, so that we can take corrective steps in each sub-sector to reduce overall energy consumption.

Electricity

In the year 2010, electricity was consumed, predominantly, in the following sub-sectors[vi, vii]

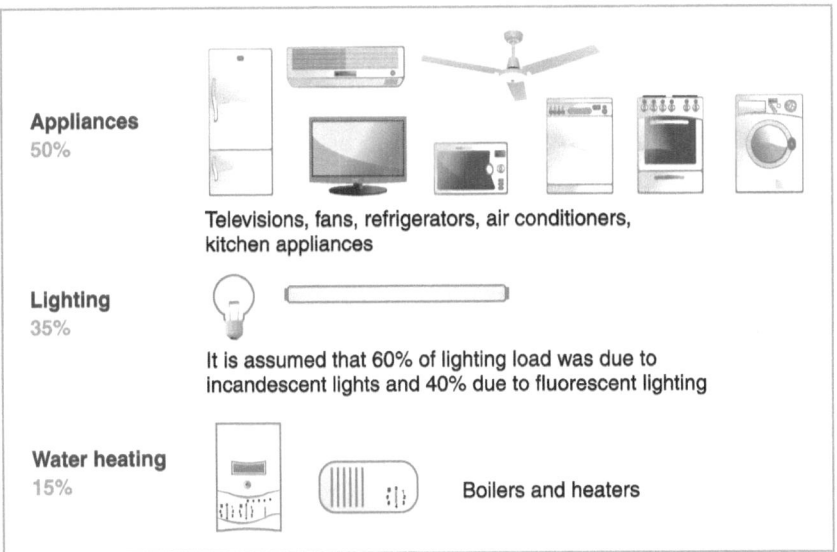

Appliances
50%
Televisions, fans, refrigerators, air conditioners, kitchen appliances

Lighting
35%
It is assumed that 60% of lighting load was due to incandescent lights and 40% due to fluorescent lighting

Water heating
15%
Boilers and heaters

Savings in Appliances

The Bureau of Energy Efficiency (BEE) operates a star-rating program that rates appliances by their energy efficiency. A higher star rating conveys higher efficiency and lower energy consumption, and lower carbon footprint.

22

To elaborate the point, take the following two examples.

Two air conditioners from the same manufacturer, from the same product line and comparable in specification and features, are compared (as per technical data of Tata Voltas products as of 2013).

One air conditioner is a BEE 2-star product and the other is a BEE 5-star product. A 5-Star product consumes less power and carries a cost premium of ₹ 5,000. **However the extra cost is paid back in form of saving in electricity bills in only 2.7 years!**[viii]

Air conditioner	5 star	2 star	Difference
Initial cost (₹)	31,690	26,690	5,000
Power (kilowatts)	1.485	1.808	-0.323
Electricity units consumed in one year (kwh)	1069.2	1301.76	-232.56
Running cost (₹)	8468.06	10309.94	-1841.88
Payback in Years			2.7

Now we consider a case of a refrigerator. As per a BEE document, a 250 litre 5-star refrigerator saves minimum 700 units of electricity annually, and prevents a minimum 560 tonnes[ix] of CO_2 annually as compared to a no star refrigerator.

Bureau of Energy Efficiency has given the following table for savings considering Electricity cost at ₹ 2.5 per unit which existed many years ago. Now the cost is more like ₹ 6 per unit! It shows that there is adequate incentive for the buyer to opt for a 5 star rated refrigerator.

Energy and Cost Saving for 250 ltrs Frost Free Refrigerator with different Star Ratings*

Rating Star Per Year (Approx.)	Energy Consumption (Approx.)	Electricity Cost /Year (₹ 2.5 / unit)	Total Saving w.r.t. No Star Every Year	Refrigerator Cost (Approx.)	Cost Difference	Pay Back Period
	kWh	₹	₹	₹	₹	Years
No Star	1,100	2,750	0	14,000	0	0
1	977	2,443	308	15,000	1,000	3.25
2	782	1,955	795	15,500	1,500	1.89
3	626	1,565	1,185	16,500	2,500	2.11
4	501	1,253	1,498	17,500	3,500	2.34
5	400	1,000	1,750	18,500	4,500	2.5

Source: Bureau of Energy Efficiency

To help moving to a 'carbon light' lifestyle, authorities should discourage sale of lower star rated appliances. The authorities should prohibit sale of inefficient appliances, just like a car is not allowed to be sold unless it follows pollution control norms. The least the authorities can do is to levy a higher VAT for less star rated appliances. A consumer guide that publishes case studies of appliances of different star ratings and associated savings would be extremely helpful to buyers who are sceptical of paying up extra money at the time of purchase. Each appliance should clearly display likely annual energy consumption for specified normal usage.

In addition to this, all star rated appliances should display a comparison table with estimated payback. The table could be as above. This will encourage a buyer to buy higher star rated appliances.

The good news is that the use of higher star rated appliances is rapidly increasing. The following graph shows that use of 5 star appliances is increasing.

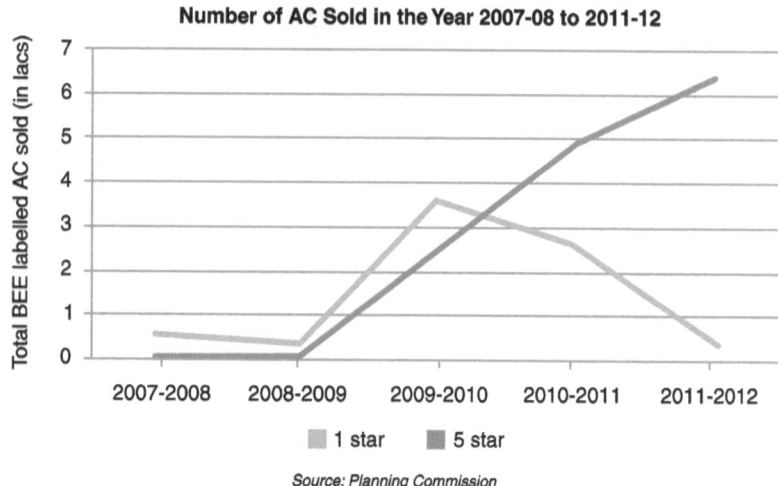

Number of AC Sold in the Year 2007-08 to 2011-12

Source: Planning Commission

We envision a scenario where all new appliance, buyers would be persuaded to buy BEE 5-star rated appliances rather than 1-star or no star appliances. Since the life of an appliance is around 7 years, by 2020, all appliances would be changed to 5-star ones. This rise in use of higher stared appliances will result in substantial saving by 2020.

Since 5 star rated appliances have 35% lower energy consumption and considering appliances account for 50% of electricity consumption, we envision a reduction of electricity consumption to the extent of 650 million units of electricity.

Use of 5 star rated appliances leads to savings of 520 kilotonnes of CO_2 every year

25

Savings in Lighting

Use of compact fluorescent lamps (CFLs) and light-emitting diodes (LEDs) would reduce domestic electricity bills substantially. **A CFL consumes about a quarter of the electricity consumed by an incandescent bulb of similar brightness, and an LED lamp consumes about half as much as a comparable CFL.**

An 11 watt CFL gives same light output as a 40 watt incandescent bulb. So it would save 29 watt power when in use. True, it costs ₹ 135 more. But assuming a daily usage of 4 hours and cost of electricity to be ₹ 6 per unit, a CFL recovers its extra cost in mere 194 days.

Energy and Cost Saving for CFL v/s Bulb

	CFL	Bulb
Consumption(W)	11	40
Running Cost (Per year)	₹ 96.36	₹ 350.4
Yearly saving	₹ 254.04	
Initial cost	150	15
Payback	194 days	

Moreover, CFLs lasts longer than incandescent bulbs. As such CFLs are financially very attractive. No incentives are required to promote their usage. It is only a matter of time before residential consumers switch over to CFLs. Some might also switch to other types of fluorescent lighting, such as energy-efficient T5 tubes. Smaller T2 tubes are also available. The efficiency of such tubes, available from a range of manufacturers, is on par with that of CFLs.

LED consumes about half as much energy as CFL. Since commercial consumers use lights for longer duration, their savings per day would be higher if they use LED. Even 20% of residential consumption may be taken over by LED depending on price of electricity in the relevant billing slab, income of user, type of usage, and so on.

We envision that 80% of domestic lighting will switch to CFL and 20% LEDs. In that case, domestic energy consumption would come down by around 54%.[xi]

Government should aggressively promote use of CFL through schemes like *'Bachat Lamp Yojana'*. In addition to this government should discourage production of incandescent bulbs. Ban on production itself will be helpful.

Bachat Lamp Yojana
Bachat Lamp Yojana is a flagship program of BEE and MNRE. Government with the help of Distribution Company distributes CFL lamps to poor household at cheaper rates. This overcomes problem of initial investment needed, which is not affordable to poor households. Further extra cost is recovered on EMI basis, included in electricity bills. The customer does not feel burden since monthly extra charge is less than reduction in cost of electricity.

Installation of motion sensors that instantly cut down on electricity usage when there is no one in the room; use of table/pedestal lamps so the entire room does not need to be lit, control switches of fans and lights located conveniently so they are switched off while leaving the room, will further reduce energy consumption.

Use of CFLs and LEDs leads to savings of 626 kilotonnes of CO_2 every year.

Water Heating

A solar water heater is a cost-effective way of reducing energy consumption and hence the carbon footprint. A 100 litre per day (LPD) solar water heater, which replaces an electric water heater consuming 3 units per day for 300 days in a year, saves 900 units of electricity and 720 kg of CO_2 per year.

Payback for Solar Water Heater

Payback	Solar Water Heater	Electric Water Heater
Initial Cost	20,000	200
Running Cost(Per year)	0	5,400
Payback	3yrs 8months	

Your investment cost of solar water heater will be recovered within 3 to 4 years. Thus no financial incentives are needed for installing water heaters. Information to assist with the retrofitting of older structures will be highly helpful to citizens who like the idea of solar water heaters, but are unaware of how to get the heaters installed at their homes.

We envision that by 2020, 30% of domestic water heating energy needs are met by solar water heaters in addition to those solar water heaters already in operation in 2010.

Improvement in the efficiency of the remaining electric water heating through better insulation and water softeners is assumed to result in a further 10% saving in water heating-related electricity consumption.

> **Use of solar water heaters leads to savings of 111 kilotonnes of CO_2 every year.**

Petroleum Fuel - LPG

LPG is used mainly for cooking. Use of microwave ovens, use of pressure cookers for cooking and use of flat bottomed pans (especially copper bottomed pans) would reduce LPG consumption by 20%. The Government may consider giving VAT and excise duty concessions to these items. To achieve this saving a time bound and targeted program is needed. LPG distribution companies along with the PMC should facilitate NGOs to conduct training and awareness programs related to 'savings in cooking'. Currently PCRA conducts such programs.

- Organized cooking activity can save about 20% energy.

- Use right quantity of water required for cooking and reduces gas / kerosene usage by 65%.

- Use pressure cooker as much as possible.

- The pressure cooker should be loaded $\frac{2}{3}^{rd}$ if the foodstuff is solid & hard and ½ if loaded with liquid.

- Properly used pressure cookers can save up to 50 to 75% of energy as well as time.

- Cook your food in solar cooker and save cost of 2 LPG Cylinders annually.

- Cook on low flame as far as possible and save 6 to 10% energy.

- Remember that a blue flame means your gas stove is operating efficiently. Yellowish flame is an indicator that the burner needs cleaning.

- Use lids to cover the pans while cooking.

- Bring items taken out of refrigerators (like vegetables, milk etc.) to room temperature before placing on the gas stove for heating.

Use of right appliances in kitchen leads to savings of 157 kilotonnes of CO_2 every year

Rooftop Solar Photo-Voltaic System

A rooftop solar PV system is used to generate electricity from sunlight.

Rooftop solar PV systems with battery and inverter can replace traditional grid power.

A solar PV system can also feed power back into the grid using 'net metering' now in vogue in many countries and even in some states of India.

A 1kW Rooftop Solar PV module costs ₹ 44,000. Add to that the cost of structure ₹ 3,000, cost of inverter and net metering device ₹ 20,000, cost of cable ₹ 4,000, and the profit for the installation company ₹ 9,000; the total cost comes to ₹ 80,000. This system would generate 5 units, on an average, per day and we expect Maharashtra State Electricity Distribution Company Ltd. (MSEDCL) to buy these 5 units at ₹ 9 per unit. That would give an income of ₹ 16,425 per year.

The owner can request a bank to give him the required loan at 10% (like a home loan) having an annual outgo less than this amount. There is thus no cash outgo during the pendency of the loan. After the loan is paid off, say in 10 years, the electricity cost will be ZERO for the next 15 years.

The earnings will go up substantially if we add benefits of
• Likely reduction in cost of Solar Panels by 50% by 2020,
• Likely increase in conversion efficiency by 2020 that would increase energy generation by 50%. A combination of these factors would make rooftop solar panels a very attractive proposition.

We envision that by 2020, 90 MW of rooftop solar PV will be installed in Pune, on 60,000 households – less than 10% of the total - each installing 1.5 kW, which will require around $30m^2$ area. This will lead to an annual generation of 164 million units. [xii]

Rooftop Solar Photo-Voltaic System

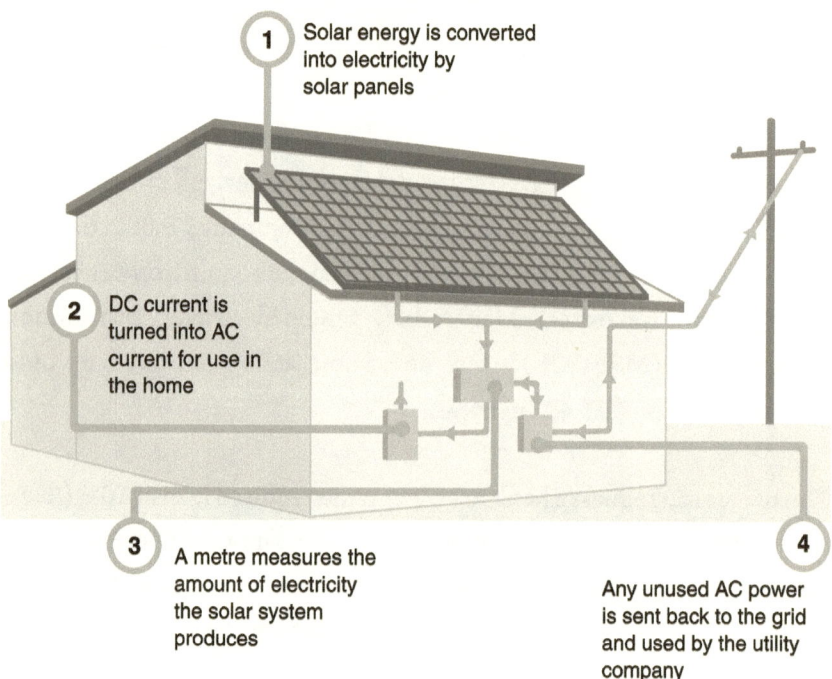

1. Solar energy is converted into electricity by solar panels

2. DC current is turned into AC current for use in the home

3. A metre measures the amount of electricity the solar system produces

4. Any unused AC power is sent back to the grid and used by the utility company

Rooftop Solar PV installation leads to savings of 131 kilotonnes of CO_2 every year

Solar Powered DC Home

This is a new concept being advocated by Prof. Ashok Jhunjhunwala of IIT Madras. It advocates that all appliances and lighting systems in a home is to be converted to DC. Power to these appliances and lighting systems be supplied by Rooftop Solar PV Systems.

Advantages
- DC appliances and lighting systems consume less energy than AC appliances and lighting systems (almost 30%) as there would be no 'inductive losses' in DC systems.

- DC appliances like a fan would consume less energy if run at a low speed whereas an AC fan wastes the energy in resistive load when the fan is run at low speed.

- AC power generation, step up transformation to high voltage, transmission, step down transformation to lower voltage and distribution involves huge losses. Some say it is almost 50%! Solar powered DC home does away with all these losses.

- Many devices like TV or computer or LED lights actually run on DC power. Feeding them with DC supply would save rectification losses that are incurred when AC power is supplied to them.

In short, a day is not very far off when solar powered DC homes will become a reality, saving huge amounts of electricity for the nation.

Green Architecture

Designing for lower energy consumption in a residence is highly dependent on building characteristics, i.e., the way our residence is constructed. Therefore, energy strategies are most effective and economical when incorporated from the earliest stages of design.

There are four types of rating and certification frameworks in India for building performance:

- IGBC Green Homes and LEED India, both administered by the Indian Green Building Council (IGBC).
- GRIHA (Green Rating for Integrated Habitat Assessment) endorsed by the Ministry of New and Renewable Energy.
- The Energy Conservation Building Code covers buildings with a minimum connected load of 100 kW.
- Star labelling scheme for energy efficiency in buildings administered by the Bureau of Energy Efficiency (BEE) under the Ministry of Power.

The ECBC will be introduced shortly for residential buildings. The purpose of these ratings frameworks is to stipulate minimum requirements for an energy efficient design and construction of building.

The following table projects energy use reduction in green buildings.

Green Building Rating Level	Energy Reduction
Platinum	40-50%
Gold	30-40%
Silver	20-30%
Certified	15-20%

In addition to energy savings 'green' buildings yield other significant benefits. They often improve resource use, incorporate on-site solid waste and wastewater treatment, and emphasize occupant comfort. In fact, all building rating frameworks mentioned, with the exception of BEE's rating system, consider these other benefits in addition to energy efficiency.

Energy Efficient Green Building

Thermal insulations

Use of alternative energy resources (solar PV panel facing south)

Reflective paint

Low emissivity windows

Trees to provide shade

Low flow and dual flush toilets

Five star appliances

Native planting (*Tulasi*)

Rain water harvesting

Compost pit

A residence, certified as per IGBC Green Homes System, provides savings of 20-30% as per the IGBC website.

Green building initiatives and design elements and techniques that can reduce energy consumption in a residence

Use of modern software

Ecotect and other similar software can guide the designer to predict and reduce the energy consumption in the building.

Site planning

Orientation of the building has a great impact on heat gain as well as ventilation. Geometrically simple, compact and open floor plans offer greater cross ventilation and cause fewer shadows in the interior space.

Material selection

Cement has a very high carbon footprint due to the energy used in its manufacturing process. On the other prefabricated materials can reduce the energy consumption in the construction process. Use of fly ash instead of cement would be an additional advantage.

Roof

Reflective roof/double roof/swimming pool on roof/sprinkler on roof/kitchen garden on roof reduce the heat energy inflow into the building. A small opening near the bottom of the protective wall around the roof allows wind flow and cools the roof.

Walls

Trombe walls or walls made of hollow bricks, cladding on the wall to be made of PCM (Phase Change Material) that will absorb the heat and not pass it on to the interior, water pipe carrying water from underground tank to overhead tank to go through the wall, climbers growing on southern walls, use of earthen materials that encourage evaporative cooling, tall trees on south side to shield the south wall from direct sunlight.

Atrium

Use atria (along with an exhaust fan/ copper plate to heat air near top of atrium) to encourage natural ventilation by stack effect using underground cool air.

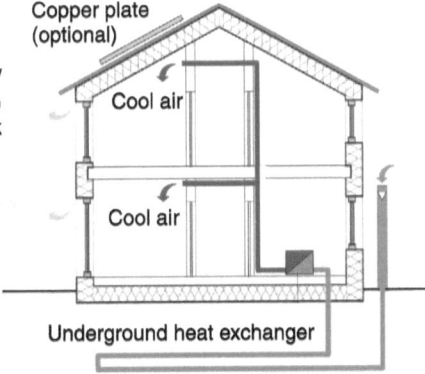

Copper plate (optional)

Cool air

Cool air

Underground heat exchanger

Windows

Retractable awnings over windows to reduce heat gain; *Khus* curtains outside the window, use of reflective glass, double windows;
All these reduce energy consumption.

Bed cooler

(like car seat cooler) working on Le Chatelier's principle would cool the bed and obviate the necessity of using an air conditioner.

Dissipates Heat

36

Reverse exhaust fan

Will bring outside cool air into the bedroom at night, obviating the necessity of using an air conditioner.

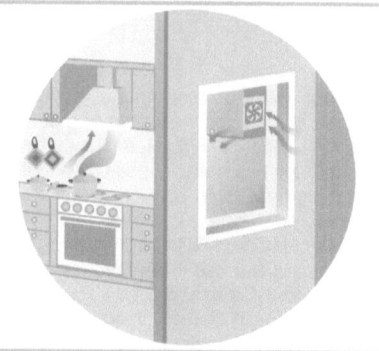

Sleeping chamber

Around a bed (of the size of mosquito net) would drastically reduce the volume needed to be cooled by air conditioners.

Mist cooling

In garden to lower the general temperature in the surroundings.

Retrofitting

Though implementation of ECBC and GRIHA rating is possible only for greenfiled projects, (i.e., projects which are newly built), retrofitting allows us to implement energy saving ideas.

To promote retrofitting we propose that PMC should give concessions in property tax for buildings with BEE star ratings. In addition, to facilitate retrofitting, PMC should follow the 'single window policy' for permission of retrofitting projects. The Pune Municipal Corporation's existing 'Eco-Housing Program' provides a strong platform to encourage the energy-conserving building design. PMC should give building permission only to green buildings with the above mentioned design elements; builders will then install these elements in the building ab initio. For the home owner it would mean a little higher EMI but lower monthly electricity bill and he would welcome it.

The Corporation should waive off Property Tax and other taxes if a building achieves target reduction in energy bill. The target should be fixed considering its area and number of residents.

There will be an increase in population by 2020[xiii] requiring new residential buildings . If the Corporation gives permission only to green architecture for new buildings we can assume that these new buildings will be 15% more energy efficient than old buildings. These savings will be due to inherent building characteristics such as building envelope, improved natural lighting, ventilation, and thermal performance, and will be distinct from savings due to efficient appliances, renewable energy installations, etc.

In case of urban renewal, old buildings giving way to new ones, this percentage could be even higher. Here we are considering a conservative value. Half of the current houses in Pune are more than 40 years old. In the next seven years these will be rebuilt. Newer buildings will be more energy efficient than the older ones. Thus savings due to green architecture will rise.

Green Architecture leads to savings of 38 kilotonnes of CO_2 every year

Behavioural Change

While technological advancement must play an important role in reducing carbon footprint, behavioural change is also an equally important variable.

Behaviour is important on many levels. A study by Anant Sudarshan[xiv] shows how sizable the savings due to behavioural change can be. It is almost equal to energy generated by windmills or biomass! And that too without any investment!

A study conducted by Sudarshan in an apartment complex in Ghaziabad found that simply letting households know their electricity consumption relative to others in the apartment complex reduced electricity consumption by 11%.

Monitoring of energy use and displaying real time cues by a red light in case consumption overshoots the target would induce the residents to instantaneously reduce energy consumption.

The human factor can be leveraged in powerful ways. For example, air conditioned buildings (which are not essential for Pune's weather) are often regulated at very low temperatures. This is often not necessary. In fact, temperature is not the only determinant of comfort. Relative humidity, wind speed, the freshness of air (expressed in a closed space as air changes per hour), and local atmospheric pressure all play a role in determining comfort. Extensive research shows that building occupants are equally comfortable at a higher ($25^{0}C$ to $27^{0}C$) range of temperatures. This knowledge can be leveraged to reduce air conditioning loads without compromising on occupant comfort.

Pune has cool nights even during summer. Installing cross ventilation systems and using outer cool air to maintain temperature can reduce consumption further. This can be achieved by using the venturi effect. Installation of a venturi fan will force outer air inside and a solar operated exhaust fan will suck out inner hot air outside and thus maintain lower temperature without any significant increase in consumption.

It is also useful to give a thought to the choice of appliances for example, the choice of a cooler over an air conditioner[xv], or the choice to use fresh foods in order to use a smaller refrigerator.

Motion sensors instantly cut down on electricity use when there is no one in the room. Use of table lamps/pedestal lamps do reduce electricity since an entire room need not be lighted, switching off of lights and fans can be controlled at one convenient point so that they are all switched off when one leaves the room.

We envision that behavioural changes will lead to a 20% reduction in the remaining energy consumption.

Behavioral changes lead to savings of 341kilotonnes of CO_2 every year.

Conclusion

Thus, by 2020, despite population and economic growth, the energy consumption and carbon footprint of Pune's domestic sector would have remained almost the same, in the 'effort scenario'.

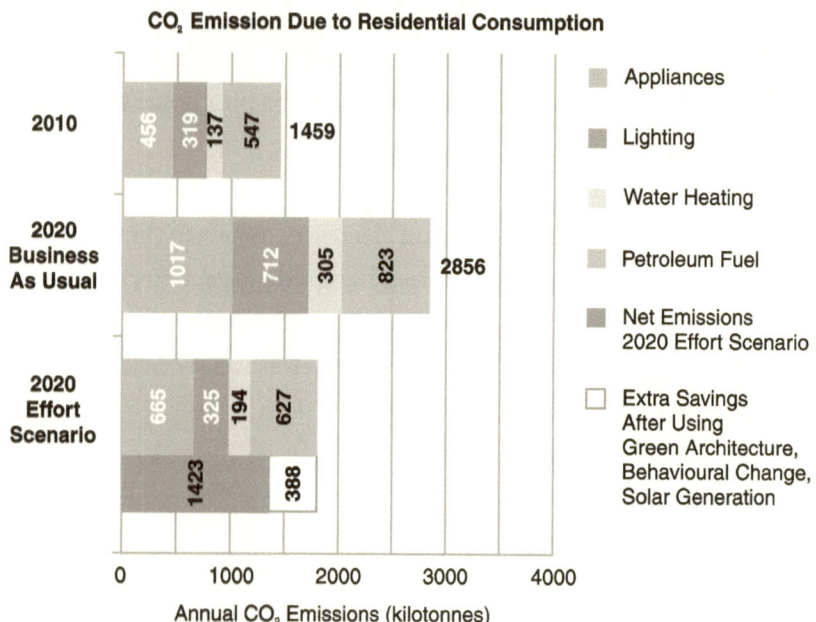

CO₂ Emission Due to Residential Consumption

2010: Appliances 456, Lighting 319, Water Heating 137, Petroleum Fuel 547, total 1459

2020 Business As Usual: 1017, 712, 305, 823, total 2856

2020 Effort Scenario: 665, 325, 194, 627, Net Emissions 1423, Extra Savings 388

Legend:
- Appliances
- Lighting
- Water Heating
- Petroleum Fuel
- Net Emissions 2020 Effort Scenario
- Extra Savings After Using Green Architecture, Behavioural Change, Solar Generation

Annual CO₂ Emissions (kilotonnes)

While helping Planet Earth by reducing Carbon Footprints, Pune residents would also be helping themselves. Reduced electricity consumption would give them a whopping saving of ₹ 17.55 billion in one year (2020) alone. And such savings will, continue every year, year after year.

> **Overall 1978 kilotonnes of CO₂ saving is possible in Domestic Consumption. This is the highest saving among sectors!**

41

Appendix

The following tables give details of residential consumption and commercial LT consumption.

	2010	CAGR	2020	2020		2020
		2010 - 2020	Business As Usual	% Reduction	Reduction Amount	Effort Scenario
Residential Consumption	Kilotonnes	%	Kilotonnes	%	Kilotonnes	Kilotonnes
1) Appliances	456	9.32	1017	35	352	665
2) Lighting	319	9.32	712	54	387	325
3) Water Heating	137	9.32	305	37	111	194
4) Petroleum Fuel						
4a) LPG	412	6.39	720	20	144	576
4b) Kerosene	135	-3.01	103	50	51	51
5) Green Architecture	0	0	0		25	-25
6) Behavioural Change	0	0	0		232	-232
7) Solar (Rooftop) Generation	0	0	0		131	-131
TOTAL	1,459		2,856		1,434	1,423

Commercial LT consumption	Kilotonnes	CAGR%	Kilotonnes	%	Kilotonnes	Kilotonnes
1) Lighting	198	10.51	486	49	240	246
2) Water Heating	0	0	0	0	0	0
3) Appliances	198	10.51	486	35	168	318
4) Petroleum Fuel						
4a) LPG	40	5.95	68	20	14	54
4b) Kerosene	0	0	0	0	0	0
5) Green Architecture	0	0	0		13	-13
6) Behavioural Change	0	0	0		110	-110
7) Solar (Rooftop) Generation	0	0	0	0		0
TOTAL	436		1040		545	496
GRAND TOTAL	1,895		3,897		1,978	1,918

[I] Year 2010 is abbreviation for year 2010-2011.

[II] Carbon Inventory of Pune City (TERI.2012)

[III] Assumed grid emission factor as 0.8

Grid Emission Factor = (sum of carbon dioxide emitted by all sources providing electricity to the grid in a given period of time)/(number of units of electricity fed into the grid by all those sources in the same period of time). This Grid Emission Factor then represents the average amount of carbon dioxide emitted due to the generation of a unit of electricity. Therefore, when electricity is consumed in Pune, it drives the consumption of coal, for example, The weighted average emission factor applicable to Pune was 0.78 kg CO_2 per unit of electricity as of 2011-12.(Page 29, Central Electricity Authority: 'CO_2 Baseline Database for the Indian Power Sector, Version 8.0', January 2013.) It could be argued that in some cases, we should be using some combination of marginal emission factors rather than weighted average emission factors; however, for the sake of simplicity, we use 0.8 throughout.

[IV] Deriving data from 'Carbon Inventory of Pune City (TERI.2012)'

[V] Prediction is based on data and assumption by 'Carbon Inventory of Pune City(TERI.2012)'

[VI] Assumptions are based on a study published by Lawrence Berkeley National Laboratory (de la Rue de Can et al, page 7) though the data is not Pune specific. We also assume that the same distribution continues until 2020 in the business as usual scenario.

[VII] For commercial consumers of LT electricity, also considered in this chapter, the split is assumed to be 50% for lighting, and 50% for appliances such as air conditioning, fans, display/TV screens, etc.

[VIII] Tata Voltas 'Luxury' 1.5 tonne window air conditioners were considered (185 LY accessed at http://www.voltasac.com/index.php?option=com_catalog&view=product&Itemid=69&id=153&cid=8&vr=323 and 182 LY accessed at http://www.voltasac.com /index.php?option=com _catalog&view=product&Itemid=69&id=142&cid=8&vr=311.

As of March 2014, the cost for the 5-star and 2-star air conditioners was ₹ 31690 and ₹ 26690 respectively). Electricity was assumed to cost ₹ 7.92 per unit, which is the electricity tariff (excluding surcharges) for the 301-500 unit monthly consumption slab.

Cost of finance/capital, has been neglected as it is assumed to be offset by the anticipated rise in electricity price (CAGR for the 301-500 unit slab in the four years from 2008-09 to 2012-13 has been 10.56%

[IX] Using, as stated earlier, a grid emission factor of 0.8Using a combined marginal emission factor (0.94), these savings would be 658 kilotonnes.

[X] http://beeindia.in/schemes/documents/ecbc/eco3/SnL/Guide%20on%20Energy-Efficient%20Home%20Refrigerator.pdf

[XI] Assuming that in the baseline scenario, 60% of lighting load was due to incandescent and 40% due to LED. The caveat here, however, is that to the extent that the demand for lighting is elastic with respect to price, higher efficiencies will be offset by higher consumption due to lower cost of lighting

[XII] 1 kilowatt of solar PV generates 5 units a day. (Plant load factor of 20.8% in 2020)

[XIII] We assume that 20% of the increase in domestic consumption and carbon footprint over the next five years will be due to increased population (This is a simple assumption based on the fact that between the 2001 census and the 2011 census, Pune's population grew at a CAGR of 1.97%. From 2005-06 to 2010-11, Pune's residential electricity consumption grew at a CAGR of 9.32% (pg 32 of TERI's 2012 Carbon Inventory of Pune City). Therefore, in the recent past, just over 20% of Pune's overall increase in electricity consumption can be attributed to population growth (with the rest due to increase in per capita consumption). All of this increased population will require living space, and therefore new residential buildings will be needed to support this population. We may therefore assume that 20% of the increase in domestic consumption will occur in new residential buildings. However, we must account for the fact that a significant portion of this new population might live in slums, where typical green architecture practices may be difficult to implement. Also, from a social equity viewpoint, the case has often been made that higher income groups should bear the cost of environmentally beneficial investments before lower income groups do. Considering these factors, and for the sake of simplicity, we exclude slums from energy savings due to green architecture. We must however keep in mind that slums would tend to be less energy intensive than regular residential constructions. We therefore assume that 15% of the rise in residential electricity consumption will be due to new residential constructions. We then assume that all the new residential constructions for supporting the additional population from 2010-11 to 2019-20, on average, consume 15% less energy than comparable buildings built without consideration to energy conservation.

[XIV] Anant Sudarshan, accessed at http://www.ideasforindia.in/article.aspx?article

Sudarshan argues that while price tools to provide an incentive/disincentive structure for such behavioural change may not be an option for politically sensitive and cash-strapped public utilities in India, behavioural and social incentives may work and, indeed, be more effective.

[XV] Desiccants can be used to address the problem of excessive humidity from such coolers.

44

Carbon Footprint for Transport

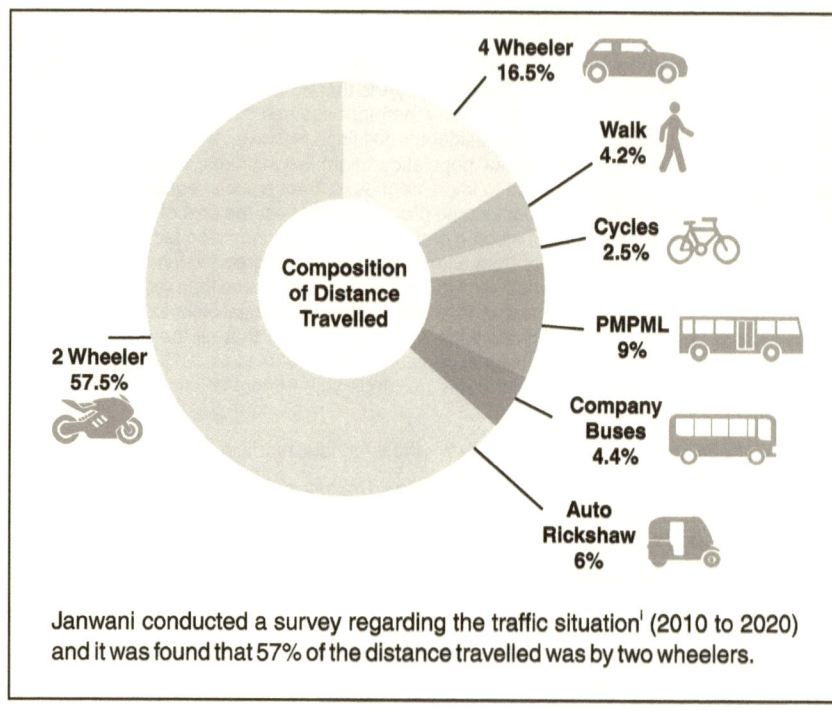

Composition of Distance Travelled

- 4 Wheeler 16.5%
- Walk 4.2%
- Cycles 2.5%
- PMPML 9%
- Company Buses 4.4%
- Auto Rickshaw 6%
- 2 Wheeler 57.5%

Janwani conducted a survey regarding the traffic situation[i] (2010 to 2020) and it was found that 57% of the distance travelled was by two wheelers.

Carbon Footprint in 2010 due to commuter travel was 741 kilotonnes of CO_2.[ii] Even if it grows only at 1.97% per year from now on in future it may go up to 1040 kilotonnes of CO_2.

Transport

Now we come to the transport sector. We are familiar with this sector too. Who is not fed up with the traffic congestion on our roads? We all sympathize with the traffic policeman who inhales all the smoke our vehicles emit. This sector is also growing rapidly and we all agree that we need to do 'something' about it. If we can bring this sector under control we will get maximum health benefits and also save money that we spent on fuel. Let us see how to go about it.

This chapter considers the carbon footprint due to travel. It broadly covers three aspects:
- Carbon footprint in 2010 and 2020
- Shift away from 'high-carbon travel' to 'low carbon travel' to go back to 2010 levels
- Shift in technology (electric and hybrid electric vehicles) that can lead to further CO_2 savings.

The sale of petrol and diesel at petrol pumps has been growing at an alarming rate, indicating that people have shifted from bicycles to motorcycles and from motorcycles to cars, and away from public transport (like bus) to private transport (like motorcycles and cars). We see thousands of motorcyclists travelling long distances to work in complete disregard to their personal safety. Can we turn the situation around?

Yes, given a will, we can.

In the past bicycle riders had shifted to motorcycles en masse. Bicycle use has now dwindled to a level that bicycle rides account for only 2.5% of distance travelled. Similarly bus travellers had shifted in large numbers to motorcycles and cars. However now we see that bus ridership has stabilized and car sales are tapering off. We envision that, in future, motorcyclists may buy cars but not use them for their daily commute. Car journeys are more time consuming due to heavy congestion on road and scarcity of vacant parking spaces. So, we assume that while people may continue to buy cars or motorcycles, passenger-kilometres would increase only as per population growth, at 1.97%. Proportion across modes would also stabilise at present levels. However, this does not serve our purpose of going back to 2010 levels. So we need a further shift to public transport and bicycle, and suggestions to achieve this are given below.

What should we do?

Charity begins at home. For reducing transport emissions, each of us has to contribute. This can be done by reducing emissions from personal vehicles. Following are some measures compiled from the 'Petroleum Conservation Research Association (PCRA)', which will help to reduce CO_2 emissions from vehicles. This will lead to increased mileage of a vehicle which will also save money.

Good Driving Habits

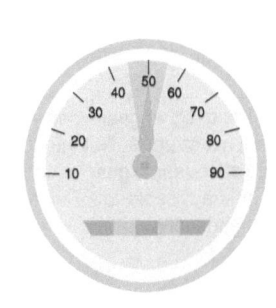

Drive between 45-55 km/h
Drive slow and steady. The faster you go, the more wind resistance your vehicle will face. If you go at speeds above 60 km/h, you will waste petrol. Tests on Indian cars prove that you can get up to 40% extra mileage at 45-55 km/h as against 80 km/h.

Remember
Avoid accelerating or decelerating unnecessarily. Avoid banking by anticipating stops and curves well in advance. Tests show that a reduction in speed leads to no appreciable rise in commuting time. Much less than what most people think.

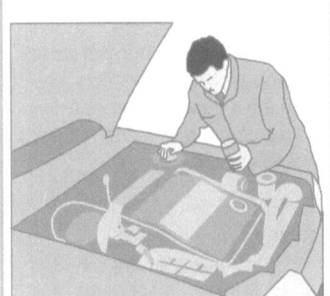

Keep your engine healthy
Tests on a large number of vehicles proved that you can save as much as 6% by tuning your vehicle regularly. If your engine emits black smoke, has poor pulling power or consumes large quantities of oil, get it checked immediately at a reputed garage. A delay may prove more expensive in terms of petrol and oil as compared to the cost of an overhaul.

Remember
Use of bi-metallic spark plugs saves over 1.5% fuel and reduces exhaust emissions too. Get your car serviced at every 5,000 km and bike at ever 3,500 km.

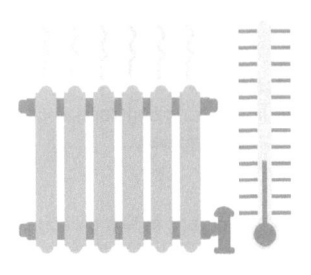

Don't wait for your vehicle to warm up
Instead, drive in low gear till the engine warms up. Use choke briefly only when necessary.

Remember
At 10°C and below, your fuel consumption per kilometre doubles when you make trips of 5 km or less. So combine trips. Do not park a car so that you have to reverse with a cold engine This will consume more fuel.

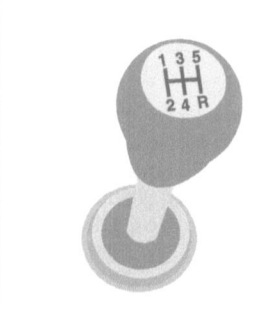

Drive in the correct gear
Incorrect gear shifting can lead to as much as 20% increase in fuel consumption. Start your car in the 1st gear only, except if you are in a muddy patch or going downhill then engage the 2nd gear.

Remember
For city driving, change to a higher gear when you are sure the engine will not struggle. Get into top gear as soon as possible. Use same gear for uphill and downhill journey. It is advisable to follow the manufacturer's recommendations.

Good braking habits
Stop-and-go driving wastes fuel. When you slam on the brakes, a lot of useful energy is wasted in the form of heat. A good driver always anticipates stops.

Remember
Test wheels for free rotation when your vehicle is being serviced. Binding of brakes restricts free wheel movement and the engine consumes more petrol in order to overcome resistance. Check wheel alignment at regular intervals.

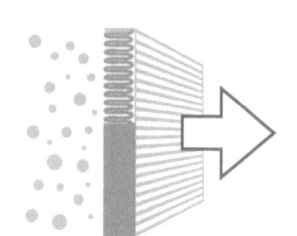

Clean air filter regularly
Air filter prevents dust from fouling the engine. Dust causes rapid wear of engine components and increases fuel consumption.

Remember
Cylinder bores wear out 45 times faster in engines without air-cleaners. Clean air filters every time-up.

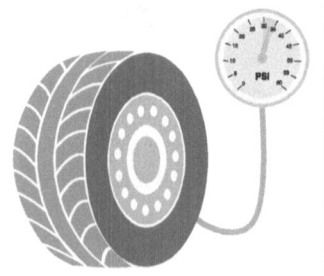

Watch your tyre pressure
Under inflated tyres increase rolling resistance, leading to higher petrol consumption.

Remember
Tests show that a 25% decrease in tyre pressure can cost you 5-10% more on petrol and 25% on tyre life. Use radial tyres for 3-7% fuel economy, longer tyre life and greater riding comfort.

When you stop your vehicle, stop the engine
Always keep your vehicle ready to start. Keep the battery, dynamo, self-starter and fan-belt in good condition. This will ensure a quick start whenever you need it.

Remember
Switch off the engine at stops of over 2 minutes for cars and 30 seconds for two wheelers.

Use the recommended grade of oil
Check the vehicle manual and oil manufacturer's recommendations, before using any particular grade of oil. Always use multi-grade oil equivalent to SPCC/SGCC type for added benefits.

Remember
Engine oil that is thicker than the recommended oil can cause 2% increase in fuel consumption. Change oil filter along with engine oil.

Plan your route
Rush hour, or stop-and-go traffic, can waste fuel excessively. You will get more mileage from each litre if you take a less congested route, even though it is slightly longer. Search for the shortest route using Google maps and plan accordingly. Google maps also show route options. Choose your option wisely.

Remember
Fuel consumption in a highly congested road can be double than normal.

Car Pool
Look for people who go in the same direction as you. You can share your car and the costs.

Plan your trips
Before you start on a trip, ask yourself two questions:
Is this trip really essential? Can I combine this trip with other trips in the same direction?

Use Public Transport

A bus emits only 10% as much CO_2 per passenger as a car (since a bus carries more than 30 passengers!). So obviously we need to increase use of public transport. That is the way to go back to 2010 levels.

Pune Municipal Transport popularly known as PMT is operating buses in the PMC limits. A fleet of about 1,000 buses transporting nearly half a million passengers in a day, a staff of about six and a half thousand, six depots, eighteen main bus stations and about 200 routes are operated and maintained by PMT. PMPML has been formed merging PMT and PCMT. Even then, the gap between transport demand and supply is increasing in Pune. Mumbai's BEST had a fleet of 1,800 buses in 1971 when it had to cater to a population of quarter million people. Pune today has roughly the same number of people (today as Mumbai did back then) but the PMPML has only about 1,000 buses in running condition.[iii] As a result, Pune has a low share of public transport and high share of private transport.

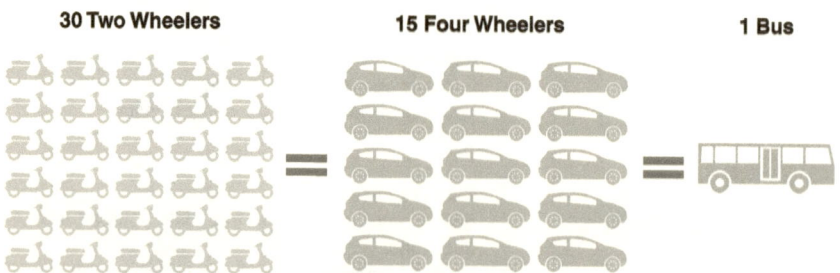

30 Two Wheelers = **15 Four Wheelers** = **1 Bus**

We all know that use of public transport will increase only when it will be reliable, trustworthy, safer and cheaper than private modes of transport. For this, following actions are recommended:

- PMPML should be given adequate funds to buy as many buses as required to meet the demand. During rush hours private mini buses may be allowed to supplement the PMPML bus fleet.

- In order to attract commuters who travel a fixed route to go to work or study, monthly passes should be issued at ₹ 400 (or 5% of minimum wage) regardless of the distance and regardless of breaks in the journey. Any revenue loss should be recovered from parking fees for car users (at ₹ 50 per hour) and motorcycle users (at ₹ 10 per hour).

- 'On time' performance should be the main criterion to judge the efficiency of PMPML. Bus fare should be refunded if the bus is delayed by more than say, 10 minutes.

- Not only quantity but quality is also important. Buses should be clean and comfortable; CNG should be used as fuel. Swiping of credit card should enable passenger to travel in the bus. Lack of availability of change should no longer be a deterrent for use of buses.

- A passenger should be able to reserve a seat in the bus he/she normally uses for going to work or school. Then friends can travel together and enjoy their bus journey.

- Buses should carry 'name boards', just like the ones we find in trains. Passengers would feel affinity to his bus, just like they feel greater affinity to a train called 'Deccan Queen' rather than 'train no. 12124 that departs at 7.15 am'.

- Colour coding of routes: Colour coding of routes will make travel simpler even for new commuters. This will also lead to integration of all routes and will build a relationship between passenger and buses.

- AMT (automatic manual transmission) should be used to reduce driver fatigue. Drivers should be trained in 'safe' driving. Conductors should be trained to be courteous.

- Solution should be found to the 'first mile/last mile' problem. i.e. how to reach the station from home. Those who come to the bus station on bicycles /motorcycles should be provided underground parking facility. Parking fee should be waived to passengers who travel long distances on the bus. Similarly at the alighting stations the passengers should be given free use of a bicycle (against the security of swiping his credit card) and again the rental should be waived if the passenger undertakes his return long distance journey by the bus.

- Bus stations should be commuter-friendly. They should give information about the expected time of arrival of next bus. It is possible if all buses are fitted with GPS system. Apps can be developed for smart phones that would tell the user where to change the bus and time to reach the destination. Janwani is already working on this.

Use Bicycles

Creating an environment conducive to bicycling can take many motorized vehicles off the roads, particularly for short to medium distance trips.

One may also wonder how to accommodate bicycles on the already overcrowded roads. For this purpose a study was conducted on Delhi Roads by Unified Traffic And Transportation Infrastructure (planning & Engineering) Centre (UTTIPEC). This showed that improper management and not obeying basic rules of traffic and parking, was the reason for wastage of the space. By proper management and demarcation, roads became safe and all accommodating. Just by ensuring parallel parking of cars and proper demarcation, all modes got accommodated on the road.

Following steps will encourage people to take to bicycling:

- Personal safety of travel is the main concern of bicyclists. To allay this concern, we need to define and create dedicated bicycle lanes. They have to be wide, well levelled, and smooth. All obstacles and encroachments on bicycle lanes should be removed or shifted. No vehicle other than bicycles should be allowed to enter in bicycle lanes.

- Even on arterial roads dedicated bicycle lanes on each side of the road could become popular, if they are made two-way. That way bicyclist won't have to go to next traffic light and make u-turns like car drivers have to.

- Some roads should be declared 'bicycle only'. Or 'Two wheelers only' with half of the road reserved for bicycles.

- *Nallah* Tracks: Janwani proposed construction of bicycle lanes on the space available on the sides of the *nallahs*. That way no demand is made on the existing roads. If these bicycle lanes originating from *nallah* tracks lead to metro stations it will solve the problem of 'last mile connectivity' for the metro. For this purpose metro stations would have to free provide underground parking for the bicyclist-commuters.

- *Nallahs* flowing through Kothrud intersects important roads. Thus there will be node points where *nallah* tracks will cross Paud road and Karve road. Traffic lights should be established at these junctions so that bicycle riders can cross the main roads safely.

- Initially, dedicated cycle lanes should be started as pilot projects, and then expanded into a network of well-marked and safe routes.

- One may wonder how we can create bicycle lanes on existing roads which are already overburdened with traffic. The answer to that is simple. Shift the cars parked on roadsides to nearby multistoried car parks and use that space for dedicated bicycle lanes.

- Safe and free parking: Safe and free parking facility has to be provided for bicycle promotions. Multistory parking nearby bus and metro stations will help in promoting usage of bicycles.

Why should I cycle?

Time is money. People tend to use faster modes of transport to save time. However, average traffic speed in Pune is 22 km/h. The lowest speed is 12 km/h at Mhatre Bridge. (Nal Stop to Senadatta Police Chowk).[iv] On the other hand, bicycle speed is also about 20 km/h. Thus there is no 'time Justification' to choose other modes of travel over bicycle. You will reach your destination on a bicycle in the same time!

Increase Walking

Mumbai residents walk more than Pune residents! 'Local Area Planning' will be a great step to encourage walking. To encourage *Punekars* to walk we need:

- Safe, spacious, uncluttered, and accessible footpaths.

- Prominent zebra crossings and pedestrian signals.

- Walking Plazas: Some areas are well suited for designation as walking only or walking-and-bicycling-only zones. A lot of these areas are dense, with slow-moving traffic.

Create Awareness

In a city with rapidly rising incomes, private vehicle ownership is more than a means of commuting - it also embodies social aspirations. We need to create awareness campaigns that ensure that buses, bicycles, parking facilities, etc, are in line with these social aspirations.

- We should create groups of passionate ambassadors. Such groups can be created through intensive education and promotional campaigns through short films and internet social media, and so on. Such groups can act as nodes around which an alternative culture is created.

- We need to influence policy in favour of public transport, bicycles and walking to counter popular craving for more and bigger roads, flyovers and parking. Policies have to be realigned according to priorities with respect to transport. That is choosing to allocate resources for walking, cycling and public transport, investing in buses rather than flyovers, is one expression of such priorities. Allocation of the precious resource of road space to bus lanes can also be example of prioritising in favour of public transport.

Ideally, pedestrians should be given highest priority, followed by cycling. Then comes public transport and in the end are private vehicles. These priorities have to be followed in all cases from allocation of resources to planning and designing.

• We can bring prominent citizens of Pune on board with campaigns for bicycles, walking and public transport. Such individuals forcefully backing practices and policies that move away from a car-dependent urban fabric will again serve as nuclei for change.

Discourage Use of Personal Vehicles

Expecting a shift away from personal vehicles to public transport before any introduction of measures to discourage personal vehicles would be naive. The incentives for public transport, bicycles and walking should be complemented with disincentives for use of personal vehicles.

• The most important action would be to shift roadside car parking and two wheeler parking to nearby amenity spaces where multistoried parking garages can be built. These parking garages should be owned by the PMC and can be leased to private operators to operate and to collect parking fees. The parking fee could be ₹ 50 per hour for a car and ₹ 10 per hour for a two wheeler. Revenue from such a move should be channelled towards promoting usage of buses, bicycles and walking. It would then increase public willingness to switch modes from private vehicles to public transport, bicycles and walking.

- Similarly, creation of dedicated bicycle lanes would reduce space available for personal vehicles, inducing a shift away from personal vehicles.

- Other factors might also reduce the use of personal vehicles. The increase in online marketing combined with home delivery means that fewer people make trips for shopping. Instead, a single trip is made, along an optimised route, for multiple deliveries.

- Rising fuel prices will encourage car-pooling. This means that for the same number of passenger kilometres, a fewer number of vehicle kilometres would be travelled.

- It is worth noting that as incomes rise, some people have multiple cars. This means that the optimally sized car would be used for any given purpose. No more must a largish single car, which also doubles up as a family picnic car, be used to commute to work.

- Finally, we can also assume that due to rising fuel prices, the ongoing trend towards efficient vehicles will accelerate.

Singapore introduced 'Vehicle Quota System' in 1989. It is a car ownership restraint policy, to reduce the pollution in the city. It limits the growth of vehicular population. Under this system, a fixed number of new vehicle entitlements are auctioned to the highest bidder each month. The price of a new medium-sized car has risen to over six times its market value. This resulted in double benefits. It arrested vehicle population and pollution and also earned handsome amount of money to government.

Savings in CO_2

As a result of incentives/disincentives we hope to achieve the following:

- Of commuters using two wheelers for medium trips (3 to 6 km), 50% would switch to public transport.

- Of commuters using two wheelers for long trips (more than 6 km), 70% would switch to public transport.

- Of commuters using four wheelers for medium trips, 30% would switch to public transport.

- Of commuters using four wheelers for long trips, 50% would switch to public transport.

Great reduction would be achieved in the city's total carbon dioxide emissions, bringing total emissions in 2020 down to 667 kilotonnes – lower than the level in 2010![v]

These actions would lead to savings of CO_2 emission of 373 kilotonnes every year.

CO_2 Emissions Due to Transport Sector

	2013	2020 (Business as Usual)	Reduction Amount	2020 (Efforts Scenario)
2 Wheelers	429.34	492.16	314.24	177.92
4 Wheelers	320.62	367.53	188.72	178.81
PMPML	61.27	70.24	-159.18	229.41
Company Buses	22.89	26.24	1.25	24.99
Autorickshaws	73.51	84.27	28.04	56.23
Total	907.63	1040.44	373.07	667.37

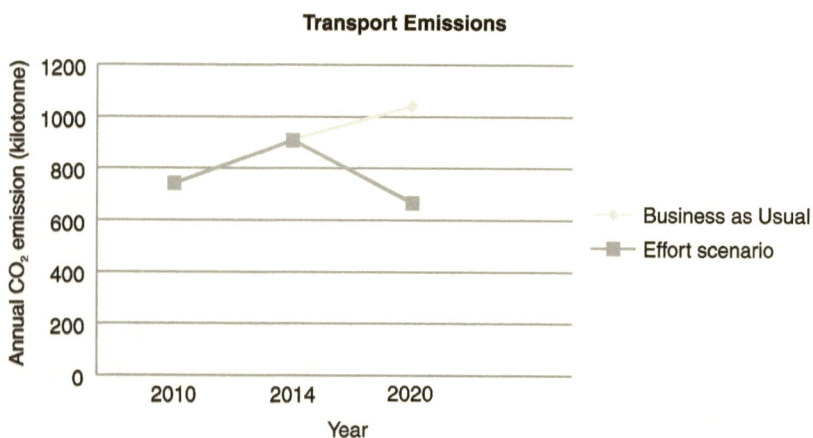

Transport Emissions

Savings in Fuel

Switching to public transport leads to very significant savings on fuel for citizens. If some of this can be recovered to be channelled towards further development of public transport, one can envision a virtuous cycle of desirable modal splits paying for themselves. It would lead to fuel savings worth ₹ 21.4 billion[vi] annually in 2020. This must be judged in the context of the fact that PMPML's annual budget stands at a few hundred million rupees.

Incidentally, the modal split achieved through such actions takes Pune almost exactly halfway from 2013 figures to the targets laid out in Pune's Comprehensive Mobility Plan (CMP), which has been approved by the General Body of PMC. Since CMP targets are to be met in 2030, getting halfway in 2020 is an important step towards fulfilling CMP's vision.[vii,viii]

Shift in Technology

Technological shift includes transport system management, capacity expansion and technological advancements. Technological advancements further target emissions, noise, fuels and safety. They also target improving existing situation by new engine or fuel technology, and look at future solutions considering alternative form of vehicles. Here we will discuss some of the ideas which will help to reduce CO_2 emission.

Electric Autorickshaws

Apart from shift to low carbon travel by behavioural and infrastructural change, we can also take advantage of technological innovation. Electric

---

CMP targets are ambitious and would result in huge reductions in CO_2 emissions, made possible by the fact that other modes of very efficient transport, such as the planned Pune metro, will be in operation by then. We have considered a less aggressive set of targets that can be achieved by 2020, without developments like the metro. The modal split that we envision will take us nearly halfway from present-day distribution to that envisioned in the CMP.

CMP envisions a total investment of ₹ 227 billion up to 2030. We envision going only half the distance up to 2020. Further, in the case of plans for Pune metro, for example, only 20% is to be borne by PMC. This translates to an annual requirement of ₹ 4-5 billion for PMC. This can be recovered through parking fees, increased property tax collection from commercial establishments, and so on.

---

and hybrid vehicles are excellent examples of such technological innovation. [ix] Autorickshaws, of which there are around 60,000 in Pune as of 2013, can be run on electricity. An autorickshaw that runs 120 km per day can be charged overnight and run on battery power. Considering an autorickshaw runs for about 120 km per day we can expect substantial savings in petroleum fuel and CO_2. This means that, by conversion of petrol rickshaw to electricity, 14% CO_2 emissions can be saved.

	Autorickshaw	
	Petrol	Electricity
Mileage (kmpl)	25	
Specific Gravity	0.74	
Mileage (km per kg)	33.78	10.4 km/ kWh
Fuel Consumed per km	0.02	0.096[x] kWh/ km
Emission Factor	3.06	0.8
Kg CO_2 / km	0.09	0.07
Ridership	1.2	1.2
Kg CO_2 / km/ person	0.075	0.064

Hybrid Electric Vehicles

Diesel transport vehicles that ply fixed distances can be hybridised and run partly on electricity and save energy. These vehicle owners can be expected to make the shift because of the low payback period resulting from the high number of kilometres run. Hybrid vehicles vary greatly in the complexity of the system and the cost associated with it. As an example here, an easy-to-install hybrid system for retrofit is considered for use in taxis that ferry commuters to work, plying along relatively predictable routes and covering large distances (~200 km) within the city every day.

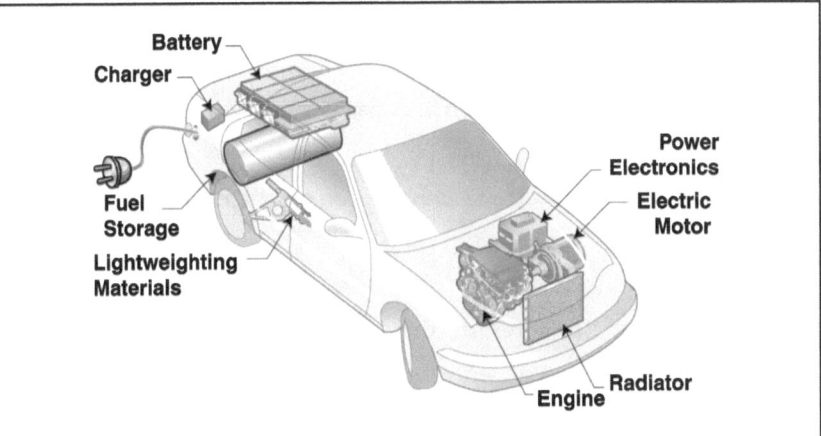

Non-plug in hybrid vehicles uses charged battery while running and uses it for lower speed. It saves almost 25% of energy for buses and 15% saving is possible for four wheelers. We envisage that, transport vehicles in Pune would be hybridized fully. This will lead to saving of 21 kilotonnes for buses, and 48 kilotonnes for four wheelers. Non-plug-in hybrid vehicles adds no load on grid and thus CO_2 savings are possible without disturbing any mode of travel and electricity grid.

Conclusion

Electric and hybrid vehicles are becoming increasingly competitive as the prices of petrol are increasing. The hybrid system described above, for example, uses the case of a 300 km per day vehicle, which is typical for about commercial 5,000 cars in Pune. In such a case, using a model where finance costs are incorporated and the battery for the system is leased, the system pays back for itself in the seventh month. Even for a vehicle that travels a hundred kilometres a day, the system pays back within three years. Support is surely required for both electric and hybrid vehicles.

- Direct subsidies, carefully calculated, can have a significant impact on adoption. The benefits in terms of energy security and balance of trade should result in substantial subsidy.

- Waiver of RTO tax, reduction in excise duty as VAT.

- Directing that fresh permits will be given only to electric autorikshaws and taxis.

- Infrastructure that supports this technology. Charging stations at parking facilities would enhance confidence in the range of these vehicles.

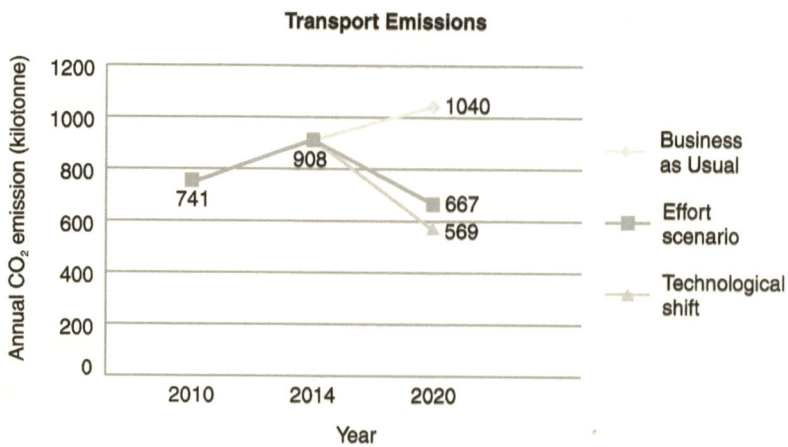

Thus additionally, over behavioural savings, shift to modern technology will save 98 kilotonne of CO_2 emissions.[xi]

Final emissions after technological shift would show saving of 481 kilotonne of CO_2.

63

How to make BRTS system successful

BRT system assumes great importance in inducing a shift from private to public transport since BRT system not only saves money for the passenger but also saves him valuable time.

- Market research should be conducted to decide the routes of highest traffic so that they can be developed into high-speed corridors such as with BRT systems (and, at future dates, metro and monorail). Frequency of buses and trains should be highest on these corridors.

- Investment should be made in pedestrian subways at BRT stations, enabling commuters to cross roads. Such subways can have licensed vendors for everyday goods, forming a sort of bazaar. This would cut down on need for the subsequent additional shopping trip by commuters. Free bicycle parking should be provided at such underground locations for BRTS pass holders.

- While BRTS has not caught on in Pune due to a number of reasons, BRT system has been a success in Ahmadabad. It has also been hugely successful elsewhere in the world, with Seoul and Curitiba often being seen as role models. PMC should study those systems and implement the steps necessary for the success of BRTS.

Public Transport Corridors

Public transport corridors are those on which high frequency of buses is maintained. These include BRTS routes as well as other non-BRTS routes.

Potential Public Transport Corridors

1. Warje to Kharadi (22km)
2. Kothrud Depot to Vishrantwadi (17km)
3. Dhayari to Hadapsar gaditil (17km)
4. Kalewadi phata to Katraj (17.5km)

These corridors are designed to service the whole city.

Comprehensive Mobility Plan (CMP):

In accordance with NUTP (National Urban Transport Program) PMC has framed CMP. It targets 50% of trips will use non-motorised forms of transport, a further 40% will use public transport, and only 10% will use private vehicles. As of 2013, as per Janwani's survey data, 34% of trips use non-motorised transport, 18% use public transport (including autorickshaws) and 48% use private vehicles.

Ahmedabad BRTS (Janmarg)

Janmarg studied and designed routes such that it covers maximum parts of the city creating a 'net'. BRTS routes act as feeder to local railway and also to metro routes. Janmarg also offered several incentives for using BRTS in technology friendly way. In Ahmedabad, BRTS and Municipal transport are operated by different companies. These companies work in coordination with each other.

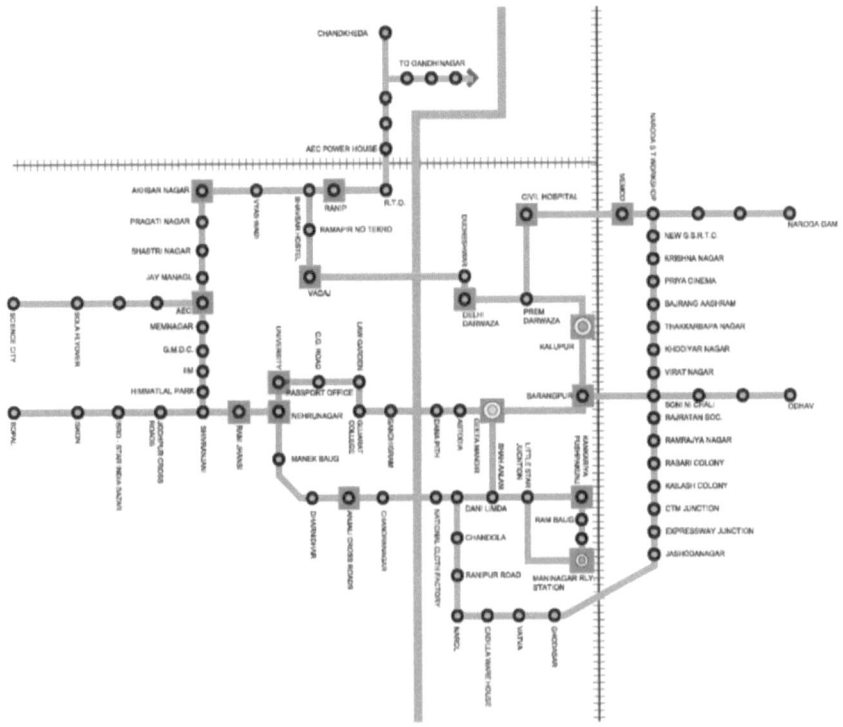

Janmarg Smart Card
Presenting Janmarg smart card with special offer

- Recharge ₹ 50 and travel worth ₹ 55
- Now travel with minimum balance of ₹ 11
- For every recharge, get 10% extra value

Local Area Planning

Local Area Planning (or LAP) is a new thought in urban planning where the master plan or a comprehensive plan of a city is also detailed at a 'local' or 'ward' or 'neighbourhood' level. There have been attempts to introduce this new level of planning in Delhi, Rajkot, and Ahmedabad so far. Janwani conducted a LAP exercise in an area between F.C.Road and J.M.Road. It is a mixed use neighbourhood. The aim of this exercise was looking closely at the local issues related to quality of life of the residents and providing short, medium and long term solutions.

In the local surveys conducted with residents and visitors, it was found that the main concerns in this study area were restricted mobility for pedestrians (with hurdles in crossing the streets especially for elderly and children) and lack of amenities such as public parks and green areas. Most other amenities such as schools, colleges, hospitals etc. were found to be easily accessible to the local residents. In the study area it was found that most needs of residents like

- Buying vegetables, milk, groceries, medicines, books, general stores etc.
- Visiting ATM
- Repairing gadgets, appliances and even vehicles.
- Visiting music, photography, fitness clubs, fast food, sweet shops.
- Children's park etc. can be met within walking and bicycling distance The need for vehicular travel is then substantially reduced.

However, the current pedestrian network is not continuous and has obstacles such as cluttered/ encroached/ broken footpaths and thus an urban intervention for a 'pedestrian network' is proposed.

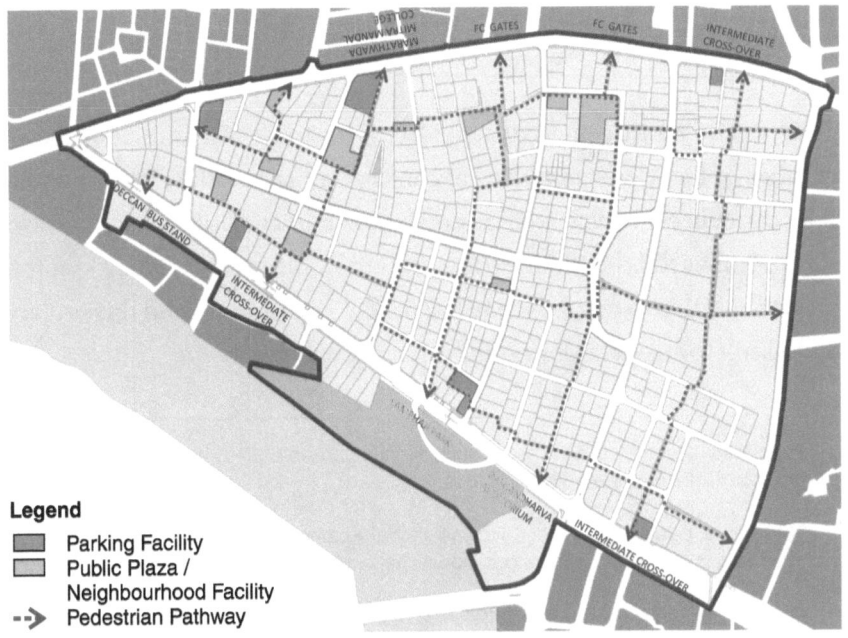

Legend
- Parking Facility
- Public Plaza / Neighbourhood Facility
- Pedestrian Pathway

A continuous pedestrian and bicycle network will make walking and cycling pleasant and safe while eliminating congestion, noise and pollution. It is suggested that the pedestrian and bicycle network is implemented through Development Control Rules. It is also proposed that the underused side margins of the current and proposed commercial or public buildings should be used as part of this network. Creating such local area plans as a level below Development Plan or Master Plan would curb use of personal vehicles for short trips.

Share a bicycle

There is also an attractive concept of 'take it and leave it' bicycles. A large number of bicycles stands can be constructed across the city. A bicycle rider can collect a bicycle from any of these stands and bring it back or leave it at any other stand. Swiping his credit card would serve as security for the bicycle and also to pay for the rental used. PMC should fund this project and lease it to an operator who will man the cycle stands.

Proposed project: Janwani has designed and proposed a 'take it and leave it' cycle project for the University of Pune campus.

75 Cycles to be distributed over 6 stations within the campus.
The stations should be able to accommodate parking facility for 15 cycles.

Operational plan: There will be different schemes to join as well as different pricing models including yearly, monthly, daily and hourly memberships with discounts and incentives. For students, the membership can be obtained through student's centre/admission department. Visitors can take it on daily or hourly basis against a security deposit.

Security mechanism: The cycles are uniquely colour coded so as to reduce theft. Also each cycle would be fitted with a GPS device to track its location at any given time.

Maintenance: The students can take the cycles to a repair shop located at the central administration office and get it repaired free of cost (air and punctures). Any large scale damage shall be recovered from the deposit paid during the membership.

The Ten Simple Rules of Urban Transportation Planning
by Hartmut Topp[xiii]

These transportation planning rules only seem to be simple; their application is indeed a difficult job. But often simplification helps in the discussion and enforcement of environmental requirements.

Rule 1: Make every effort to accommodate the real needs of people. Do not forget the children, the elderly and the disabled. Prepare your plans and programs in cooperation with the public concerned. Urban planning and transportation planning is a social, psychological, economical, ecological, architectural and engineering job.

Rule 2: The prosperity of a city does not depend on private car traffic, but on accessibility in general, on the amenity of its streets and open spaces and – to put it more succinctly – on its genius.

Rule 3: Transportation and land use must be balanced. Mixed land use must be achieved to reduce journey distances. High density with mixed land use is effective from a transportation point of view. But don't go beyond the limits of the rule.

Rule 4: Mathematical modelling of traffic behaviour and traffic volumes is an important preparation for the decision making. But don't stretch it beyond its limited validity.

Rule 5: Observe the environmental ranking of transportation modes: walking is preferable to cycling, cycling is preferable to public transit, and transit is preferable to private car traffic.

Rule 6: Urban streets are open spaces for the general public. Consider all functions of the street - social life, strolling around, providing access to buildings, as well as being a transportation facility for pedestrians, cyclists, public transit and private car.

Rule 7: With increasing density the needs of traffic regulations and their enforcement grow rapidly. Strict area-wide parking restrictions are the most effective measures to control traffic.

Rule 8: Most important, especially in high density areas, is urban design and architecture according to human scale. The design quality of a street helps to compensate for the environmental impact of car traffic.

Rule 9: The ground level of streets has to be primarily designed for pedestrians and cyclists, including wide sidewalks, bike lanes, and crossways over the driving lanes.

Rule 10: Provide more plantings and trees within the streets, including facade and roof planting, thus opening the sealed street.

Appendix

[I] Survey was conducted by Janwani in 2013; Janwani's data only considers passenger information, data on commercial traffic is not captured. Therefore we assume that 20% of diesel goes to long-distance buses and trucks, and 20% goes to within-city HCVs, LCVs, and diesel gensets

[II] "Carbon Inventory of Pune City' (TERI, 2012), petroleum sales data

[III] Comprehensive Mobility Plan; Pune Municipal Corporation (Page 4-21)

[IV] CMP (Page 4-11)

[V] If these targets are achieved, a reduction of 35.9% is achieved in the city's total petroleum consumption by weight, along with a 35.9% reduction in carbon dioxide emissions. This would translate to 373 kilotonnes of carbon dioxide savings annually in 2020.

[VI] Assuming a 2013 fuel price of ₹ 50 per kg for CNG, ₹ 58.28 per litre for diesel, ₹ 77.25 per litre for petrol, annual price rise of 7%, and annual growth in number of fuel consumption (in the baseline scenario) of 1.97 % (population growth rate).

[VII] Pune's Comprehensive Mobility Plan (CMP) envisions that 50% of trips will use non-motorised forms of transport, a further 40% will use public transport, and only 10% will use private vehicles. As of 2013, as per Janwani's survey data, 34% of trips use non-motorised transport, 18% use public transport (including autorickshaws) and 48% use private vehicles.

[VIII] In this chapter we have focussed mainly upon passenger transport. Commercial (goods) transport is not considered.

[IX] Below are some calculations to indicate the relative carbon intensity of a typical small petrol vehicle and a Mahindra Reva e2o, an actual electric vehicle available in the market.

Conventional Internal Combustion vehicle (small car, 14 kmpl actual fuel efficiency)

	CAR			
	Petrol	Diesel	Electricity	
Mileage (kmpl)	14	13		
Specific Gravity	0.74	0.83		
Mileage (km per kg)	18.91	15.49	7.4	km per kWhr
Fuel Consumed per km	0.05	0.064	0.135	kWhr per km
Emission Factor	3.07	3.18	0.8	
Kg CO_2 / km	0.162	0.20	0.108	

(Specific gravity and emission factors from 'Carbon inventory of Pune city: TERI 2012', page 42 Electric Vehicle (Mahindra Reva e2o) Battery specifications and range for Mahindra Reva were obtained from a review of the vehicle conducted at http://www.team-bhp.com/forum/official-new-car-reviews/134857-mahindra-reva-e2o-official-review.html. (10 kWh battery;74 km per full charge; 0.135 kWh per km)

As per this, an electric vehicle emits around 33% less than a conventional vehicle (0.162 kg vs. 127 kg CO_2 per km travelled). Note the CEA data for grid emission factors does not include transmission and distribution losses. However, the scope of this report excludes transmission and distribution losses, For a more detailed discussion of the rationale for this scope, see TERI, 2012: Carbon Inventory of Pune City, section 2.1.2 on page 21 and section 3.3.2 on page 25

	Bus		
	Diesel	CNG	Electricity
Milage (kmpl)	3	3.5	0.666
Specific Gravity	0.839	0.185	1
Milage (km per kg)	3.575685	18.91892	0.666
Fuel Consumed per km	0.279667	0.052857	1.501502
Emission Factor	3.1863	2.6928	0.8
Kg CO_2 / km	0.891102	0.142334	1.201201
Ridership	25	25	25
Kg CO_2 / km/ person	0.035644	0.005693	0.048048

[x] With reference to (http://www.bajaj-auto-rickshaw.com/msg.php?id=99), typical electric auto consumes 9.6 units of electricity for 100 km travel. Motor is of 1000W, 48 V thus rated current would be 20.8 A. Thus battery of 200AH will last for 9.6 hrs. Thus total consumption would be 9.6 units. This gives 0.096unit per km travel.

[xi]

		Savings possible	Kilotonne CO_2
Additional savings Due to Technological shift	Electric Rickshaws	14%	7.87Hybrid
	PMPML	25%	57.35
	Hybrid Company Buses	25%	6.25
	Hybrid Private cars and taxies	15%	26.82
Total			98.30
Final emissions possible after technological shift			569.07

[xii] http://www.ahmedabadbrts.com

[xiii] Hartmut Topp, Dipl.-Ing. is Professor (a.D.) of Transportation Planning at the University Of Kaiserslautern, Germany. He is one of Europe's foremost transportation planners, having led the transportation planning movement that began in Europe in the 1970s to calm traffic, encourage biking and transit, create pedestrian networks, and make streets once again hospitable to all pedestrians.

This summary, first published in the IMCL Newsletter February 1987, was presented at the 1st IMCL Conference in Venice, Italy, 1985.

Carbon Footprint for Institutional Consumption

CO_2 Emissions in 2010 And Likely in 2020 In The 'Business as Usual' Scenario[i]

	CO_2 Emission in 2010	CO_2 Emissions in 2020 'Business As Usual'
Public works - Electricity	229[ii]	273
Public works - Methane emissions	332	396
Large private consumers- Electricity	1,005	1,946
Industrial petroleum	245	640
Total	1,812	3,255

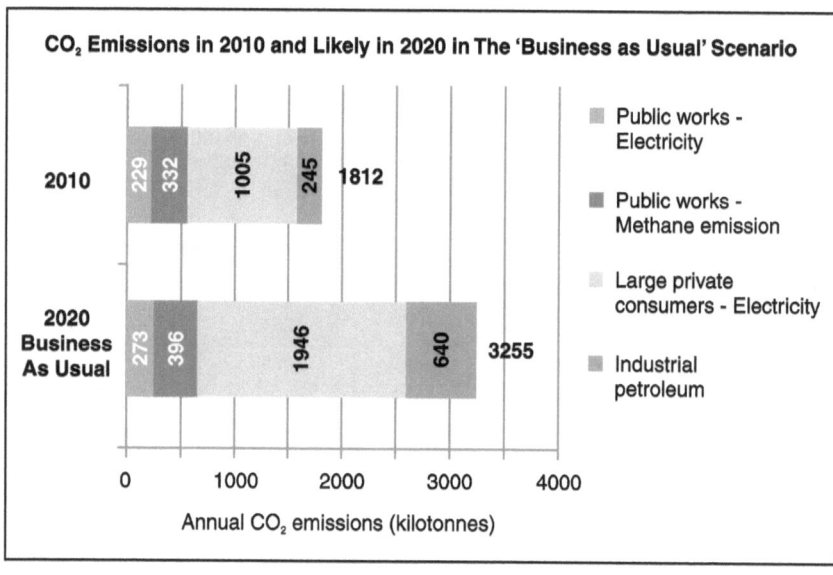

CO_2 Emissions in 2010 and Likely in 2020 In The 'Business as Usual' Scenario

2010: 229, 332, 1005, 245, 1812

2020 Business As Usual: 273, 396, 1946, 640, 3255

Annual CO_2 emissions (kilotonnes)

- Public works - Electricity
- Public works - Methane emission
- Large private consumers - Electricity
- Industrial petroleum

Institutional Consumption

In this chapter we will study the carbon footprint due to institutional consumers, i.e., public works and large private consumers[iii]. We will analyse two aspects:

- Carbon footprint in 2010 and 2020
- Shift from 'high-carbon way' to 'low-carbon way' so as to go back to 2010 CO_2 emission levels

Multiplexes, shopping malls and offices are coming up everywhere. They are all air conditioned and need huge amounts of electricity. Providing electricity in a low-carbon way is a big challenge before us. Similarly, industries will grow and consume more electricity and petroleum fuel. Providing for their growth in a low carbon way is yet another challenge.

Public Works

98% of electricity consumption for public works is due to three activities:

- Street lighting
- Water treatment plants (including pumping)[iv] and
- Sewage treatment plants.

Together these consumed, 281 million units of electricity in 2010, resulting in 225 kilotonnes of CO_2 emissions. Additionally, solid waste disposal and sewage in the city resulted in about 332 kilotonnes of CO_2-equivalent of greenhouses gases, specifically methane.[v]

Street Lighting

Good news first. PMC has been actively pursuing efficiency in street lighting[vi], beginning with a pilot in 2006-2007. What should PMC do next? A study suggests that through regular cleaning of street light luminaries, using Constant Light Output Controllers, and lights designed to adapt to traffic density situations, can save 54% of electricity.[vii] These are low cost but has high yield saving. LED street lighting in the next big thing for the PMC to do.

LED Street Lighting

Light-Emitting Diode (LED) technology is developing at a rapid pace. LEDs yield further savings (up to 50%). LED lighting is far better than that

Comparison Between High Pressure Sodium Light (HPS) and LED Street Light

Items	High Pressure Sodium Light - HPS	LED Street Light
Photometric Performance	Bad	Excellent
Electric Performance	Electric Shock Easy (High Voltage)	Safe (Low Voltage)
Working Life	Short (5,000 hours)	Quite Long (>50,000 hours)
Power Consumption	Quite High	Quite Low
Startup Speed	Quite Slow (Over 10 minutes)	Rapid (2 seconds)
Optical Efficiency	Low	High
Color Index / Distinguish Feature	Bad, Ra <50 (The Color Of Object Is Faith, Boring, Hypnosis)	Good, Ra >75 (The Color Of Object Is Fresh, Veritable And Comfortable)
Color Temperature	Quite Low (Yellow or Amber, Uncomfortable)	Ideal Color Temperature (Comfortable)
Light Pollution	Strong	No
Heating	Serious (>300°C)	Cold Light (<60°C)
Maintenance Cost	High	Quite Low
Product Weight	Heavy	Light
Cost-Effective	Low	High
Integrated Performance	Bad	Excellent

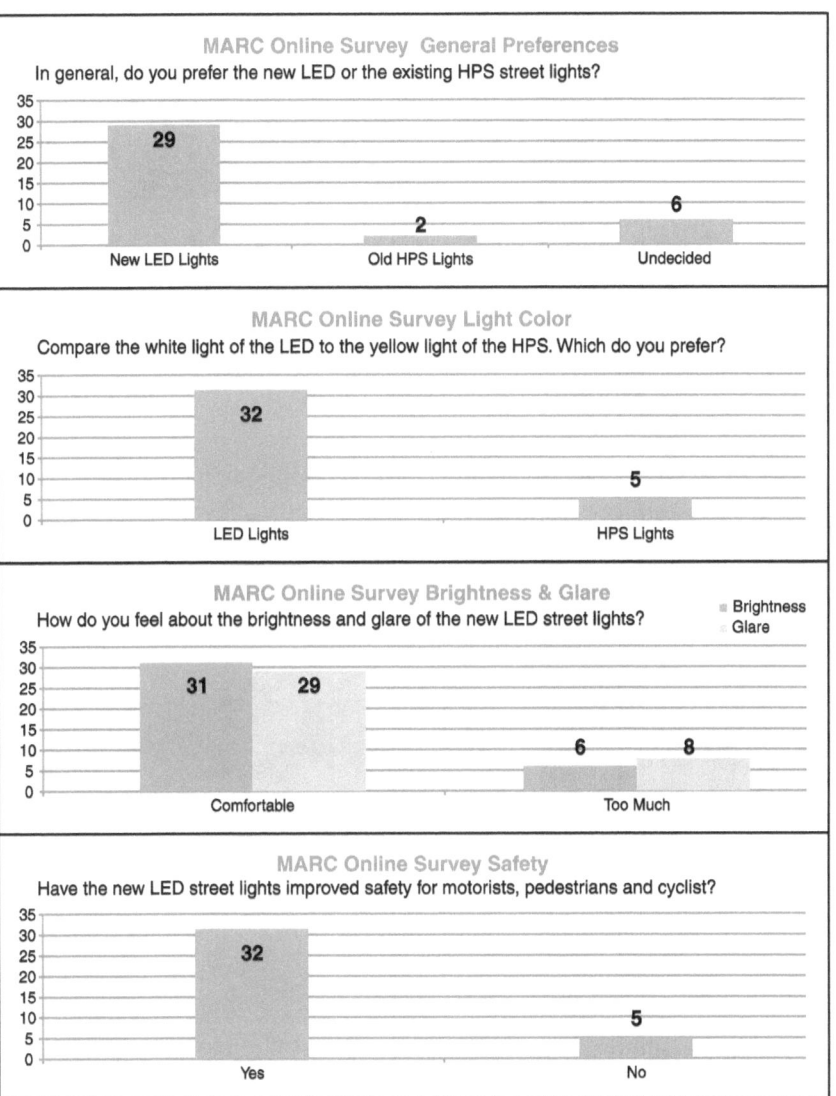

MARC Online Survey General Preferences
In general, do you prefer the new LED or the existing HPS street lights?

New LED Lights: 29
Old HPS Lights: 2
Undecided: 6

MARC Online Survey Light Color
Compare the white light of the LED to the yellow light of the HPS. Which do you prefer?

LED Lights: 32
HPS Lights: 5

MARC Online Survey Brightness & Glare
How do you feel about the brightness and glare of the new LED street lights?

Brightness
Glare

Comfortable: 31 (Brightness), 29 (Glare)
Too Much: 6 (Brightness), 8 (Glare)

MARC Online Survey Safety
Have the new LED street lights improved safety for motorists, pedestrians and cyclist?

Yes: 32
No: 5

'Smart lights for smart city' study was carried out by Mid-America Regional Council (MARC). It installed 5,753 streetlights across 25 American cities as pilot project. These installations are made through public-private partnerships. Report concludes that LED street lights are not only energy efficient but also aesthetically pleasing.

> **It is suggested that Pune should convert all street lighting to LED technology by 2020. We envision that 50% savings in electricity consumption by this measure. This leads to savings of 20.51 Kilotonnes of CO_2 every year**

HPS (High Pressure Sodium)lamps currently in use. Not only that, LED lamps also contribute to street safety and are aesthetically pleasing.

Water Pumping

Water pumping is the largest consumer of public works energy. Water demand is projected to increase to 960 MLD for 2021 as seen below, needing even more electricity.

Future Water Requirements[viii]

Year	Projected population PMC	Projected population Pune Cantonment	Total population	Water requirement (MLD)
2011	3,115,431	79,965	3,195,396	671
2021	4,487,573	87,962	4,575,535	960
2031	6,211,404	95,959	6,307,363	1,324
2041	8,597,417	10,3956	8,701,373	1,827

Source: VSPL Calculations, 2012

How to reduce electricity consumption in water pumping?

- Firsts we should accurately map water supply network and setup a defect reporting system. That would help us identify leakages, which is where a loss of water pressure occurs. Plugging such leakages would yield very substantial savings. Recent reports cite that the water loss due to leakages in tanks and pipes is between 25% and 40%.[ix] Therefore, at least that amount of pressure loss, and therefore electricity consumption, can be averted.

- Regular energy audit of water pumping stations and implementation of advanced energy efficiency measures. 'Alliance to Save Energy' and PMC had jointly conducted such experiments at Parvati Pumping Station, which proved to be useful.

- Water recycling would reduce demand for water thereby reduce need for electricity for pumping it. Garden and car washing can use locally recycled water after local treatment

- Pricing of water according to what it actually costs to supply would induce the residents to minimise wastage of water.

- Additionally, an intensive education campaign should be launched. That would help in making the residents start conserving water.

- A more ambitious project can be considered. Pune receives water from Panshet and Varasgaon dams, which are situated at relatively high altitude. However, their water is first allowed to come down to the lower level of Khadakvasla dam, from where it is pumped to supply the city. An alternative can be the direct delivery of water by overhead pipes from Panshet and Varasgaon dams to overhead tanks of the city (in the western parts of the city, at least).^{x} That would not only save pumping load but may even generate significant amount of electricity.

We envision that all these measures would lead to an overall 50% saving in water pumping related electricity consumption. This leads to savings of 77.47 kilotonnes of CO_2 every year

Sewage Treatment

Sewage treatment is a huge problem in Pune, the installed capacity for sewage treatment falls short of sewage generated. Untreated sewage leads to emissions of methane, a potent greenhouse gas.

Decentralized treatment of sewage is a promising solution to solve the installed capacity shortage problem. Enzymatic process and bio-remediation (using plants to remove sewage load) to treat sewage locally at the level of a housing society, for example, would significantly reduce the load on municipal sewage treatment plants. All water leaving such properties (if not reused within the same property for gardening) should be required to meet PMC guidelines.

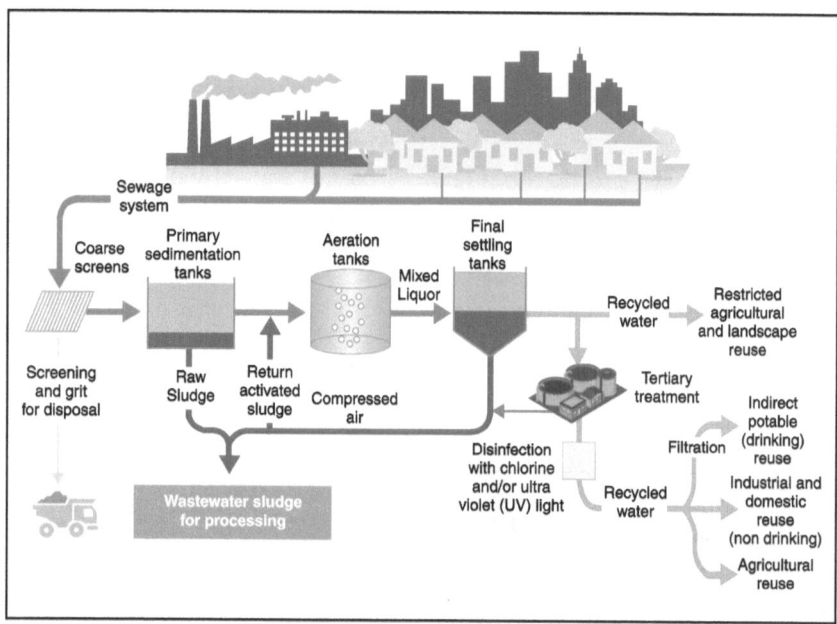

New constructions must be required to treat sewage on-site. Not only that, even the existing constructions should be encouraged, via a progressive set of incentives and mandatory regulations, to adopt the same water-treatment technologies over a period of a few years. That will greatly take sewage treatment load off the PMC footprint.

Complementing the municipal sewage treatment plants by society level or ward level sewage treatment gives the advantage that the methane emissions from untreated sewage would get eliminated.

Methane

Sewage produces methane. It has high Green House Gas potential (21 times that of CO_2!). Thus methane emission needs to be avoided.

On the other hand, methane has very high calorific value. If trapped, methane could be of great use to combustion and power generation. It is also an excellent source of hydrogen, which can be used in fuel cells to generate electricity!

Power vehicles

Household food waste and sewage

CNG after scrubbing

Generates electricity

Provides heat

Processed by anaerobic digestion at sewage works

Biogas produced

We envision that the methane emissions from sewage will go down by 30% in 2020. This leads to savings of 42.64 Kilotonnes of CO_2-equivalent every year

Municipal Solid Waste

PMC is well on its way to replicate the 'Zero Garbage Katraj' model across Pune city. It is carrying out intensive outreach programs to bring citizens on board with the vision for a garbage-free, low-carbon Pune. This project will be fully implemented well before 2020. This will lead to complete stoppage of dumping and storing of wet waste and elimination of associated greenhouse gas emissions. Dealing with waste at the ward level will also reduce emissions associated with transporting solid waste.

Implementation of Planning Commissions Guidelines

The Planning commission has laid down guidelines for urban waste disposal. It recommends scientific waste disposal techniques and segregating the waste at source. This model of waste management needs to be implemented by PMC in coordination with NGOs, industries and most importantly, citizens of Pune. These targets have to be achieved till 2017. We expect 100% achievement of targets which will help in emission reduction.

Target Set for MSW Management In the Twelfth Plan

Parameters	Benchmark
Household Level Coverage	100%
Collection Efficiency of MSW	100%
Segregation of MSW	100%
MSW Recovery	80%
Scientific Disposal of MSW	100%
Cost Recovery of SWM	100%

We envision that the methane emissions from MSW lying around and rotting will be completely eliminated in 2020. This leads to savings of 253.60 Kilotonnes of CO_2 (equivalent) every year.

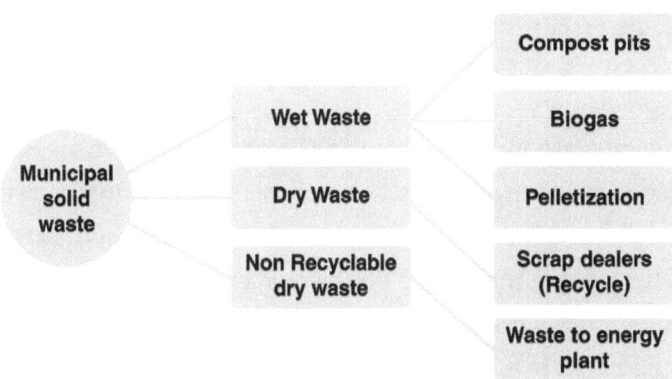

Zero Garbage Project
A Janwani Initiative

The Zero Garbage model addresses the two key challenges faced by every city in India that is collection and segregation of waste. A pilot of the Zero Garbage model was implemented at Katraj Ward No. 141.

Janwani partnered with the PMC, the wastepicker cooperative SWaCH, Cummins India and others to develop and implement the model. The public-private partnership developed a new system for waste management in the city.

Reducing the garbage sent outside the ward by processing it within the ward itself is the primary objective of the model. Wet waste is processed within the ward thereby reducing the transportation cost and saving money. The DRY garbage is collected by the wastepickers who sell it to the scrap dealers for recycling. Since minimum garbage is sent outside the ward, so the name of the project is "ZERO GARBAGE".

The important indicators of Zero Garbage Ward Model are
100% door step collection
100% segregation of garbage

Stakeholders in the Zero Garbage Ward Model

Pune Municipal Corporation (PMC) Solid Waste Management		Collection agency Door-to-door collection of waste
	Janwani Facilitator	
Households and Commercial units Segregate the waste into dry and wet waste		Corporate Volunteer / Sponsor Financial assistance and volunteering

Waste to Fuel

Pune generates around 1000 tons of wet waste per day. This waste can be converted to pellets, which can be combusted for cooking. These pellets are especially useful in establishments like restaurants, hospitals, etc, where a steady heat supply is required. Pune would then reduce LPG usage by 24 kilotons per year. This is over 13% of Pune's annual LPG consumption, and would result in a carbon saving of 72.5 kilotons of carbon dioxide annually. We can assume that half of Pune's wet waste in 2020 will be diverted to pelletization and save 36 kilotonnes of CO_2 annually.

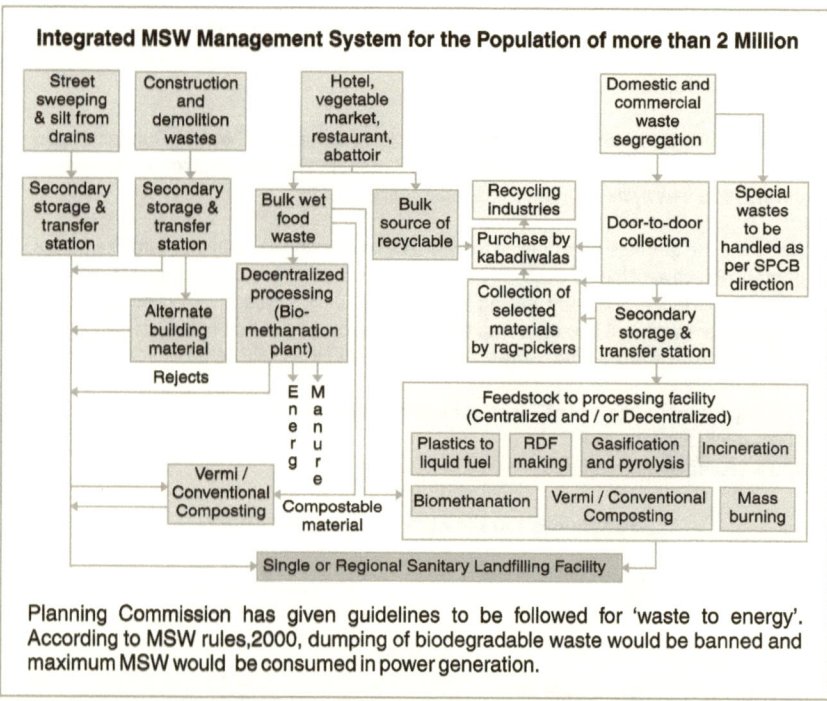

Integrated MSW Management System for the Population of more than 2 Million

Planning Commission has given guidelines to be followed for 'waste to energy'. According to MSW rules, 2000, dumping of biodegradable waste would be banned and maximum MSW would be consumed in power generation.

This will lead to savings of 36 Kilotonnes of CO_2.

Miscellaneous Public Consumption

Miscellaneous public consumption mainly includes electricity consumption in public buildings. This can be reduced by implementation of 'green building' ideas. If all governmental buildings would be BEE star rated or IGBC certified, not only will CO_2 emissions be saved but a new trend will be established.

In addition to this, government departments should buy only five star rated appliances. The government is generally the biggest customer. If the government sets a standard of buying only five star rated appliances, then a huge demand for efficient appliances will be triggered and research in energy efficiency will get a kick start.

A dedicated approach in energy savings, particularly in building savings, will yield savings in miscellaneous public consumption. These emissions will be crucial since, it will encourage savings by people at large.

Large Private Consumers

Commercial Building Savings

The Bureau of Energy Efficiency's Star Rating for commercial buildings has set different criteria for office buildings, hotels, hospitals, retail malls and IT parks. Across these different building types, and two relevant climatic zones, a typical 5-star building consumes around 45-60% of a 1-star building. [xi] The following table shows possible energy savings for star rated commercial buildings.

Star Ratings and Energy Use Intensity Norms by BEE

Climatic Zone	Composite	Warm and Humid	Hot and Dry	Temperate
A. Day Use Office Building				
Less than 50% air conditioned built up area				
1 Star	80-70	85-75	75-65	
2 Star	70-60	75-65	65-55	
3 Star	60-50	65-55	55-45	
4 Star	50-40	55-45	45-35	
5 Star	Below 40	Below 45	Below 35	
More than 50% air conditioned built up area				
1 Star	190-165	200-175	180-155	
2 Star	165-140	175-150	155-130	
3 Star	140-115	150-125	130-105	
4 Star	115-90	125-100	105-80	
5 Star	Below 90	Below 100	Below 80	
B. Shopping Mall Building				
1 Star	350-300	450-400	300-250	275-250
2 Star	300-250	400-350	250-200	250-225
3 Star	250-200	350-300	200-150	225-200
4 Star	200-150	300-250	150-100	200-175
5 Star	Below 150	Below 250	Below 100	Below 175

Zero Carbon Energy by Large Private Consumers

Large private consumers like shopping malls, multiplexes, office buildings and even industries consume large amounts of electricity. So they are looked upon as 'wasteful' users of 'precious national resource' like electricity which is in 'short supply'. This issue can be solved if such consumers are asked to generate their own power in a 'zero carbon' fashion.

Presently open access policy is being implemented across the country by electricity utilities. It allows consumers to purchase electricity generated from any source. Suppose a large consumer (or a group of consumers) invest in a zero carbon power plant like hydroelectric plant or windfarm or solar PV farm and generate electricity there, he can receive it at Pune through the national grid. It is suggested that the government should offer substantial incentive for such a venture.

We can anticipate that 600 Million Units can be generated using this incentive. This can be achieved through a hydroelectric power plant of 114 MW (having a Plant Load Factor of 0.6) or a number of solar photovoltaic plants of total 345 MW of solar (at a PLF of 0.2) or other combinations. Tata Power has put up a 3MW plant at Mulshi near Pune. Maybe these plants can be replicated over fallow lands in and around Pune.

This provision of generating energy by carbon neutral way privately will save 480 kilotonnes of CO_2.

Conclusion

The following chart shows, sector by sector, how we can reduce CO_2 emissions in the year, 2020 to the level of year 2010 in spite of continued rise in standard of living.

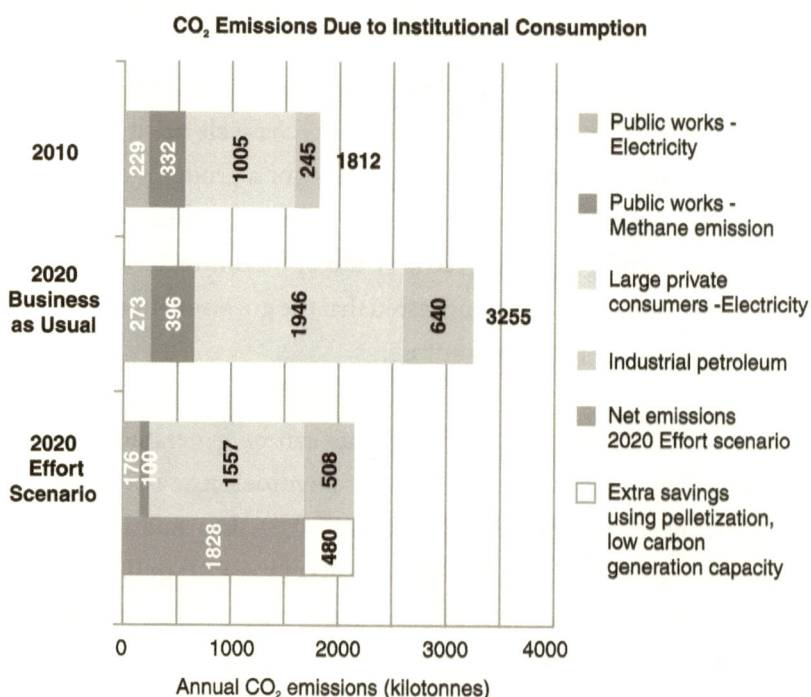

CO_2 Emissions Due to Institutional Consumption

Legend:
- Public works - Electricity
- Public works - Methane emission
- Large private consumers - Electricity
- Industrial petroleum
- Net emissions 2020 Effort scenario
- Extra savings using pelletization, low carbon generation capacity

2010: 229, 332, 1005, 245, 1812

2020 Business as Usual: 273, 396, 1946, 640, 3255

2020 Effort Scenario: 176, 100, 1557, 508; 1828, 480

Annual CO_2 emissions (kilotonnes)

Overall Large Private Consumers (Commercial and Industrial) would yield savings of 997 Kilotonnes of CO_2

87

Energy audit and advisory services conducted by experts would help commercial consumers to realise significant savings. The following steps are recommended:

- All large consumers like malls and multiplexes (say 1 MW and above) should be asked to comply with 5 star rating of BEE. Those who fail to adhere to this stipulation should be charged electricity at a higher rate, say ₹ 12 per unit.

- Green architecture techniques that include passive and active systems, for lighting, ventilation and occupant comfort should be applied successfully in commercial spaces.

- Switching lighting to LEDs can yield enormous savings. This also makes financial sense, given that commercial users pay high rates per unit of electricity. Mandate that new commercial buildings above a certain size have LED fixtures.

- Depending on available rooftop space, solar powered air conditioning should be used, with an ammonia-based vapour absorption cycle.

- Some commercial units, such as eateries, have hot exhaust air. Waste heat can be captured through heat exchanger to power vapour absorption cooling units.

- We realise, however, that not everybody might adopt these strategies. While new buildings can offer very high savings, most buildings are pre-existing buildings. Therefore we envision that all put together and averaged across commercial bulk consumers, 20% savings would be realised due to such energy efficiency measures.

Industrial savings
- The IGBC code can help casual observers to identify an industrial facility as environmentally friendly, which can act as benchmark for energy efficiency. The CII - Sohrabji Godrej Green Business Centre building is the first platinum-certified building in India. Mahindra Reva's Bangalore plant is also platinum-certified.

- Industries are well-suited to Solar PV electricity generates and consumption, because they pay, on average, higher rates for electricity as compared to residential consumers. They can also use the benefit of accelerated depreciation. Therefore for them the payback period for solar PV systems is very attractive. Control panels, lighting, some compressors, pumping and cooling needs can be good applications for solar energy.

- Compact floor plans help to reduce distribution losses , location of machinery consuming large electricity near HT/LT transformer, use of thicker cables and better switches can yield savings up to 5%.

- Maintenance of Unity power factor by using Automatic PF Correction Capacitors can reduce energy bill and also qualify a unit to get a refund of 7% from MSECDL!

• Use of a smaller capacity transformer at night (when power demand is low) will reduce no load losses at night.

• Compressed air is wasted to atmosphere after use whereas hydraulic oil is put back into the tank. So hydraulic power should be used where possible rather than pneumatic. If pneumatic power is required, screw compressors should be used. They are more efficient. Compressed air pipelines should be of large diameter and should have minimum bends. Pressure regulators and air guns should be used on all air pipes. Can yield savings up to 10%.

• Frequency converter drives reduce speed of motors during idle phase. They should be fitted on all machines consuming high energy intermittently. Can yield savings up to 5%.

• Appropriately sized energy efficient motors reduce energy consumption up to 5%.

• Day lighting and energy-efficient artificial lighting for large industrial floors can yield savings up to 5%.

• Wherever possible, co-generation should be implemented that can yield sizeable benefits.

• Water pumping loads can be reduced by process water and waste water recycling at ground level and by rainwater harvesting.

• Replacing oil fired furnaces with electrical furnaces would save energy since induction heating is energy efficient.

• Waste heat can be used in Vapour Absorption cycle for chillers and air coolers.

• Sterling engine can be run on waste heat and convert it into usable mechanical energy. This can be coupled with alternator for electricity generation. Sterling engines have high efficiency and technology is already proven. There is need to ensure mass production to make them cheaper.

• Appropriate air-fuel ratio at burners would ensure efficient combustion. Efficient combustion not only reduces emissions and fuel requirement but also reduces maintenance.

• Furnace oil usage can be reduced by using high efficiency burners and using insulation on vessels carrying liquids. Precision temperature controllers can also help.

National Mission On Enhanced Energy Efficiency (NMEEE)

Several government initiatives helps industrial sector to follow energy efficient techniques. National Mission in Enhanced energy efficiency is one of those.

Under the National Action Plan for Climate Change (NAPCC), NMEEE is one of the eight missions. The objective of this mission is to perform energy conservation and mitigation of GHG emissions activities with a market based approach, allowing cost-effective technological strategies.

NMEEE has four broad initiatives to include:

Perform Achieve and Trade (PAT):
A market based mechanism to enhance cost effectiveness of improvements in energy efficiency in energy intensive large industries and facilities, through certification of energy savings that could be traded.

Market Transformation for Energy Efficiency (MTEE):
Accelerating the shift to energy efficient appliances in designated sectors through innovative measures to make the products more affordable.

Energy Efficiency Financing Platform (EEFP):
Creation of mechanisms that would help finance demand side management programs in all sectors by capturing future energy savings.

Framework for Energy Efficient Economic Development (FEEED):
Developing fiscal instruments to promote energy efficiency

We envision that well-planned and widespread adoption of measures such as those described above will reduce overall consumption of electricity and other fuels by institutional consumers by 1427 kilotonnes of CO_2. This will be second largest after domestic consumption savings! And will constitute 37.7% of total savings .

Appendix

	2010	CAGR	2020	2020		2020
		2010 - 2020	Business As Usual	% Reduction	Reduction Amount	Effort Scenario
Public Works	kilotonnes	%	kilotonnes	%	kilotonnes	kilotonnes
Street Lighting	34	1.97	41	50	21	21
Water Pumping	30	1.97	155	50	78	78
Water Treatment	44	1.97	53	0	0	53
Sewage Treatment	16	1.97	19	0	0	19
Municipal Solid Waste	213	1.97	254	100	254	0
Methane Emissions from Sewage	19	1.97	142	30	43	100
Miscellaneous Public Works (2% of total)	5	1.97	5	0	0	5
Pelletization	-	-	-	-	36	-36
Total Public Works	561		669	-	430	239

Large Private Consumers (Commercial and Industrial)	kilotonnes	%	kilotonnes	%	kilotonnes	kilotonnes
Electricity	1005	8.00	1946	20	389	1557
Industrial LPG	89	12.86	263	20	53	210
Furnace Oil	142	11.39	376	20	75	301
Light Diesel Oil	14	-25.85	1	20	0	1
Addition of ow-carbon generation capacity	–	–	–	–	480	-480
Total Large Private Consumers (Commercial and Industrial)	1250		2586		997	1589
Total Institutional Consumption	1812		3255		1427	1828

[I] The growth rate for electricity consumption for public works is assumed to be same as population growth rate i.e. 1.97%. For Large Private Consumers (Commercial and Industrial) growth rate is determined from the TERI inventory for 2007-08 to 2010-11, i.e. 8%, and extended to the future.

As of 2010, methane emissions from MSW and sewage were 213 and 119 kilotons of carbon dioxide-equivalent respectively. Increasing at the same rate as population, in 2020, emission from MSW and sewage combined will be 396 kilotonnes of CO_2 equivalent.

[II] TERI's carbon inventory states on P 34 that street lighting accounted for 43.02 GWh. It is further stated in Figure 9 that 15% of power consumption was due to streetlight feeders.

Therefore, total electricity consumption is (43.02/0.15) GWh, or 286.8 GWh. Multiplying by a grid emission factor of 0.8 gives the carbon dioxide figure in the table.

[III] All electricity and fossil fuel consumption data in this section taken from TERI (2012): Carbon Inventory of Pune City .As seen in TERI's 2012 Carbon Inventory of Pune City, The total high-tension consumption amounted to about 1,395 million units. commercial consumption accounts for 494.48 million units, and industrial consumption accounts for 152.87 million units. Since commercial LT consumption has already been considered in the domestic chapter, we consider LT industrial consumption here.

[IV] Since Figure 9 in TERI's Carbon Inventory does not explicitly include water pumping, we assume that pumping is included within water treatment plants.

[V] TERI (2012): Carbon Inventory of Pune City

[VI] A pilot study along with TERI http://www.wisions.net/files/uploads/SEPS_Summary_Lighting_India_SB037.pdf

[VII] The Electrical and Electronics Association of Malaysia (February 2012): "Technical Report: Suitability of LED For Road Lighting in Malaysia", Edition 1, accessed at http://www.mgbc.org.my/Resources/LED/Technical-Report-Suitability-of-LED-for-Road-Lighting-in-Malaysia-TEEAM-20Feb2012.pdf

[VIII] Development Plan, Pune Municipal Corporation

[IX] http://timesofindia.indiatimes.com/city/pune/PMCs-tunnel-vision-blocks-water-supply-plans/articleshow/12077575.cms;http://archive.indianexpress.com/news/civic-body-grapples-with-water-loss-due-to-leakage/934796/

[X] Electricity for pumping from Khadakvasla is technically used by the Irrigation Department rather than PMC, but is nonetheless included, regardless of bookkeeping of savings accrual.

[XI] BEE (2009): scheme for bee star rating for office buildings: details of the scheme for rating of office buildings, february, 2009; and BEE (2011): scheme for BEE star rating for shopping malls: details of the scheme for rating of shopping malls, january, 2011.

[XII] TERI Carbon inventory for Pune city report (fig 9) states WTP(including Pumping), STP, and street lighting consumption as 98% of total that is 281.064 GWh. Paragraph 2 of page 34 of the same report states 225.58GWh consumption for the same quantity excluding water purification (including pumping). Therefore water treatment consumes (281.064-225.58) GWh= 55.484 GWh. Multiplying it by 0.8 (grid Emission Factor) gives CO_2 emission as 44.387 kilotonnes.

Carbon Footprint for Pune

	CO_2 emission in 2010 (kilotonnes)	CO_2 emissions in 2020 'Business As Usual' scenario (kilotonnes)	CO_2 emissions in 2020 efforts scenario (kilotonnes)
Domestic Consumption	1895	3897	1918
Transport	741	1040	667
Institutional Consumption	1812	3255	1828
Total	4448	8192	4407

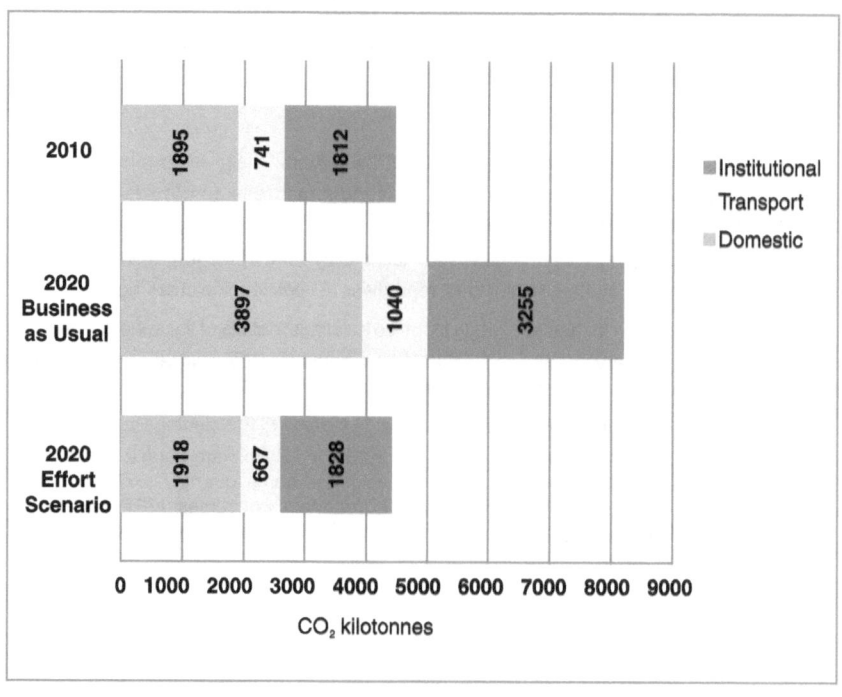

Yes, It Is Possible

Yes, it is possible to reduce the CO_2 emissions dramatically, and go back to 2010 levels of CO_2 emissions. If we all work for it, we can achieve that target.

Where Shall We Begin?

Let us begin with initiatives that cost very few Rupees per tonne of prevented CO_2 emissions.

- **Behavioural Change**

The costs here are negligible. Only creation of awareness and spreading education are necessary. Even here, expensive campaigns are not necessary. Smart pricing, smart dissemination of information that can act as a 'trigger' for behavioural change, and targeted campaigns can greatly affect the energy consumed, as discussed in the domestic consumption chapter.

- **Cleaning of Street Lamp Luminaires**

Here too, the cost is negligible. Teams to clean street lamps can be deployed on electric lifts to work on all the lamps in the city.

- **Shift Away from Carbon Intensive Travel**

Passenger information systems: Cost is low and would induce people to use public transport.

Bicycle/walking lanes: Cost to only ₹ 1-2 lakhs (100 thousand to 200 thousand) per kilometre.

94

This is the cheapest way to encourage Pune residents to avoid using personal vehicles and opting for a viable, convenient, safe, and indeed pleasant alternative.

- **Eliminating Methane Emissions from MSW and Sewage**

Again, the cost of implementing this program is very low. Such programs have already been implemented on a pilot basis, and need to be scaled up throughout the city. A nominal user fee (amount to about a rupee per day per household, combined with self-sustaining waste processing technologies and processes can avert very substantial methane emissions.

With adequate and holistic planning, these steps can be implemented almost immediately.

What Steps Should Pune Residents Take?

Domestic Sector
- Change lighting to CFL / T5 / LED
- Buy only 5 star rated appliances
- Use microwave ovens, pressure cookers, flat bottomed pans
- (especially copper bottomed pans)
- Use solar water heaters
- Instal solar generator on rooftop and feed electricity into the grid
- Stay in 'Green Home'
- Achieve energy reduction and qualify for property tax rebate

Transport Sector
- Walk wherever possible
- Use bicycles for short trips
- Use public transport for daily commute
- Use electric autorickshaw and taxi
- Convert your car to hybrid car

Institutional Sector
- Harvest rainwater
- Use water frugally
- Use recycled water for gardening and car washing
- Treat sewage on site using bio-remedial/enzymatic process
- Segregate garbage into 'dry' and 'wet' and hand over to collector at the doorstep
- Save electricity in factory / office / shop wherever one is working

What Steps Should the Authorities Take?

Domestic Sector

- Offer VAT concessions for LEDs
- Levy higher VAT for less star rated appliances
- Offer VAT concessions to microwave ovens, pressure cookers, flat bottomed pans (especially copper bottomed pans)
- PMC to give building permission only to Green Buildings having green design elements.
- For existing buildings, PMC should waive off property tax and other taxes if such buildings achieve target reduction in energy bill. Target should be fixed considering its area and number of residents.
- Maharashtra Government should allow net-metering (Tamil Nadu has already done so). Net metering means allowing residents to feed electricity generated by solar panels instantly back into the grid.
- Electricity Regulatory Commission to significantly increase the electricity tariff on higher electricity consumption slabs.
- Awareness and education initiatives to showcase model homes that can demonstrate real benefits for the residents.
- Domestic lighting-related savings as well as behavioural savings will require investment mostly in awareness and education. Such campaign should be funded. Short films, celebrity endorsements, and easily understood visual educational material are some of the media that can be used to reach key stakeholders.
- For consumers who are deterred by the upfront cost notwithstanding savings, schemes that involve utilities providing 'loans' that are recovered from electricity bill savings can be effective as well as practically cost-neutral.

Transport Sector

- PMC should develop high-speed, high frequency corridors for BRTs .
- PMPML should be given adequate funds to buy as many buses as required to meet the demand.
- During rush hours private mini buses may be allowed to supplement the PMPML bus fleet.
- 'On time' performance should be the main criterion to judge the efficiency of PMPML. Bus fare should be refunded if the bus is delayed by more than, say, 10 minutes.
- Buses should be clean and comfortable; CNG should be used as fuel. Swiping of credit card should enable passenger to travel in the bus.
- 'First mile/last mile' problem (How to reach the station from home): Those who come to the bus station on bicycles /motorcycles should be provided underground parking facility. Parking fee should be waived for passengers who travel long distance on the bus. Similarly at the alighting stations the passengers should be given free use of a bicycle (against the security of swiping his credit card) and again the rental should be waived if the passenger undertakes his return long distance journey by the bus.
- Pedestrian subways at BRT stations would enable commuters to cross roads. Such subways can have licensed vendors for everyday goods, forming a sort of bazaar. Free bicycle parking can also be provided at such underground locations for BRT pass holders.
- Subsidised passes for long distance travel will encourage long distance travellers to shift to public transport.
- Parking policies: Roadside parking should be banned. Instead parking facility should be offered in multi storeyed parking lots at appropriate fees. Amenity spaces should be used for such parking lots. The rational pricing of parking can generate revenues to strengthen public

transport by upgrading fleets, route rationalisation, and operational improvements. Shift to public transport will generate fuel savings, by 2020, of over ₹ 21.39 billion annually. Public transport strengthening can be financed by recovering some of these savings - in other words, a shift in modal split can be achieved at little net cost.

- Bicycling: Safety of travel is a bicyclist's main concern. We need to define and create dedicated bicycle lanes. A straightforward solution is to shift the cars parked on roadsides to nearby multistoreyed car parks and use that space for dedicated bicycle lanes. Free parking should be provided for bicycles near or under bus stations, entertainment centres, offices and other public congregation hubs.

- 'Take it and leave it' bicycles: PMC should fund this project and lease it to an operator who will man the cycle stands.

- Walking: Wide uncluttered footpaths should first be provided. Amenity spaces should be used for parking and meeting most of the everyday needs; that would encourage people to walk.

- Electrification and hybridisation of vehicles is the other major initiative that should be undertaken. Electric or hybrid vehicles should be exempted from permits and road taxes. In order to realise significant savings, the electricity for such vehicles should be derived from renewable sources that have been installed specifically with a view to supplying to electric vehicles. Charging facilities should be provided at all parking lots and operators of parking lots should be allowed to sell electricity to the owners of such cars.

- CO_2 emission should be taxed: A large (but modern) engine of a car would not emit much traditional pollutants (CO, HC, SOx, Nox, PM) but would emit large amounts of CO_2. Since our aim is to control CO_2 emission, it is proposed to tax CO_2 emission as well. The amount of tax could be based on star rating issued by a testing agency such as ARAI. Revenue from this tax could be used to subsidise bus transport.

Institutional Sector

- All street lighting should be converted to LED.
- Leakages in water supply system should be plugged.
- Water metres should be installed at all water connections.
- Water recycling should be made mandatory while giving permission for new buildings.
- Pricing of water should also be reconsidered. It should match the total cost of water delivery.
- Additionally, an imaginative education campaign would help in changing the mindset of Pune residents, encouraging them to start conserving water.
- Direct delivery (by pipelines) of water from Panshet and Varasgaon dams to overhead tanks in the city should be considered.
- PMC should study, approve and issue guidelines and inspection and certification procedures for enzymatic process (using enzymes) and bio-remediation (using plants) to remove sewage load locally.
- New constructions must be required to treat sewage on-site. Further, existing constructions should also be encouraged to adopt sewage treatment technologies.
- PMC should replicate the 'Garbage-free Katraj' model across Pune city by 2020.
- Land should be made available for further segregation of dry waste into 'recyclable' and 'non-recyclable'.
- Wet waste conversion to pellets / gas / compost at society or ward level should be encouraged.
- All large consumers like malls and multiplexes (say 1 MW and above) should be asked to comply with 5 star rating of BEE. Those who fail to achieve 5 star rating should be charged electricity at a higher rate, say ₹ 12 per unit.

- Energy Audit should be made mandatory for all large consumers.
- BEE guidelines for energy efficiency should be publicised, along with sector-specific examples of technologies, designs, and practices that realise savings.
- Investment allowance and accelerated depreciation: Central Government should offer to encourage investment in low-carbon electricity infrastructure. To complement this, prices for bulk consumers from the grid must be high enough to reflect the scarcity of electricity and to encourage such investment.

The major part of savings in CO_2 emissions comes from 'public awareness' as you can see below.

	1	2	3
	Savings possible with public awareness	Savings possible with administrative interventions (through guidelines and rules)	Savings possible with government's financial interventions (through subsidies and fiscal expenditure)
Domestic	1,347	631	0
Transport	251.48	186.53	-64.95
Institutional	517	215	695
Total	2,115.48	1,032.53	630

Global Benefits

The well-being that will be associated with such actions will not be restricted to residents of Pune alone. Since the greenhouse effect is a global phenomenon, the benefits from averted climate change will be shared with other countries and other regions of India (some of which, like coastal cities and agricultural areas, are both critical to the nation's economic stability and highly vulnerable to climate change).

Health Benefits

Reduced petroleum consumption will also lead to fewer pollutants like particulates, carbon monoxide, hydrocarbons, and sulphur and nitrogen oxides. This is desirable from the point of view of the health of Pune residents. The Chest Research Foundation has conducted a study in Pune which revealed that the rate of childhood asthma has doubled in the last five years. These findings were alarming enough. Such calamities will be averted if petroleum consumption is reduced.

Entrepreneurial Benefits

Many of the technologies referred to here are innovative in nature. For example, waste to wealth, solar electricity generation, energy efficient buildings, electric autorickshaws, hybrid cars, etc. They provide an opportunity for entrepreneurs, manufacturers, architects, and a broad range of other professionals to showcase their talents and can position the city as a prime destination for investment in sustainable technologies. They also offer an opportunity for economic and industrial revival and innovation in a sustainable direction.

Economic Benefits

These emission reductions also offer great cost savings for Pune residents. Savings from electricity alone would be ₹ 26.51billion every year.[i] Add to that the savings of Petroleum Fuel of around ₹ 29.65 billion every year, and it adds to a whopping ₹ 57.20 billion (almost US $ 1 billion) - more than the budget of Pune Municipal Corporation. This is explained in the table below.

Source	Amount Saved	Financial savings ₹
LPG	71 kilotonnes	8.27 billion[ii]
Petrol	180 million litres	22.92 billion[iii]
Diesel	-10 million litres	-970 million[iv]
CNG	-7.1 million kg	-570 million[v]
Furnace Oil	24.08 kilotonnes	1.04 billion[vi]
Electricity	2,403 GWh	26.51 billion[vii]
Total		57.20 billion

Conclusion

Simple and do-able! So let us do it.

It is clear what the future will look like in the 'Business as Usual' scenario, i.e., without any action. It is also clear that we have the ability to make a huge change, and steer our city's future in a different direction. It is our responsibility, as joint stakeholders in our city's future, to make the right choices.

Appendix

[I] Assuming average electricity price in 2010-11 of ₹ 6 per unit, and a conservative 7% price rise year-on-year.

[II] Assuming ₹ 63 per kg in 2010-11, 7% price rise annually to 2019-20.

[III] Assuming petrol price of ₹ 77/l in 2013, rising 7% annually.

[IV] Assuming diesel price of ₹ 58.28/l in 2013, rising 7% annually.

[V] Assuming CNG price of ₹ 50/kg in 2013, rising 7% annually.

[VI] Price of furnace oil as of 28th march 2014 by http:// www.petroleumbazaar.com/ display nationalprice.aspx

[VII] This is using the example of hydroelectricity. Hydroelectricity costs around ₹ 8 crore per MW (for example, a recent transaction where 1300 MW of hydro power was bought for ₹ 10,500 crore - http://www.business-standard.com/article/companies/jaypee-hydro-to-sell-two-hydro-projects-to-taqa-for-rs-10-500-crore-114030100175_1.html). Each MW generates around 5.26 million units per year (at a capacity factor of 60%, which is typical; for example, see http://powermin.nic.in/JSP_SERVLETS/jsp/Hydro_faq.htm). At ₹ 5 per unit, the breakeven period is just about three years. This will, of course, vary depending on the type of energy (hydro, wind, solar, etc.) used. Please note however, that if open access is used and industries use the power they generate to substitute the power they would otherwise buy from the state utilities, then ₹ 5 per unit is a significant underestimate. Instead, the rate would be higher and the payback period would be even shorter.

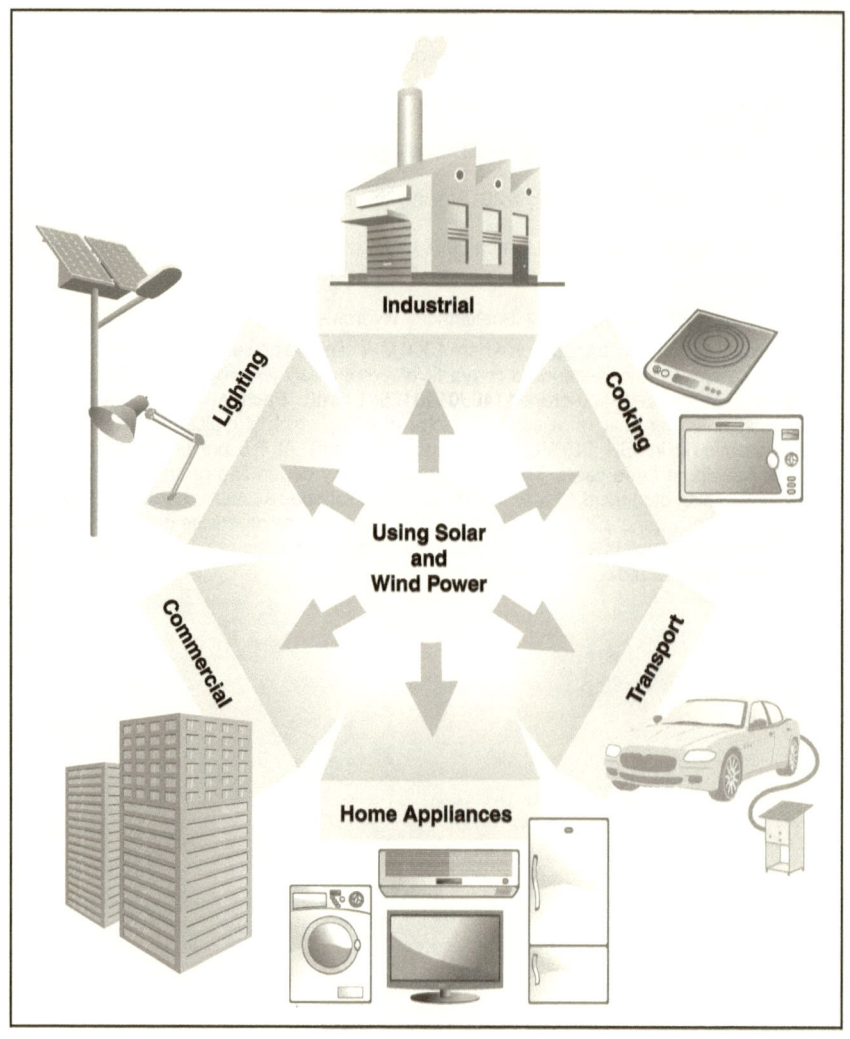

Industrial

Lighting

Cooking

Using Solar
and
Wind Power

Commercial

Transport

Home Appliances

LET US AIM HIGHER
Carbon Neutral Pune
Using Solar and Wind Power

So far, we have considered reducing CO_2 emissions to the 2010 levels. Can we aim higher? Can we aim for a carbon neutral Pune? Maybe we will have to put in heroic efforts. But is that feasible at all? The answer is yes. In this chapter we will discuss how to realise a carbon neutral Pune.

What is Carbon Neutrality ?

Carbon Neutrality means reducing net CO_2 emissions to zero. It can be achieved by three actions:
- reducing energy consumption by improving usage efficiency
- generating energy by 'clean' technologies like solar, wind, etc., and
- neutralising carbon emissions by absorbing them elsewhere.

Carbon neutrality is the one of the crucial step in sustainability. Copenhagen is planning to achieve it by 2025.

Can Pune beat Copenhagen to it and achieve it by 2020 ?

Copenhagen has declared targets in four areas:[i]
- Energy consumption
- Power production
- Transport and mobility
- City administration

Targets for Energy Consumption

- 20 % reduction in heat consumption.
- 20 % reduction of electricity consumption in commercial enterprises.
- 10 % reduction of electricity consumption in households.
- Installation of solar cells corresponding to 1% of electricity consumption in 2025.

Targets for Power Production

- District heating in Copenhagen to be carbon neutral.
- Electricity production to be based on wind and biomass and should exceed total electricity consumption in Copenhagen.
- Plastic waste from households and businesses to be separated.
- Bio-gasification of organic waste should be undertaken.

Targets for Mobility (Transport) Sector

- 75% of all trips in Copenhagen to be on foot, by bike or public transport.
- 50 % of trips to work or school in Copenhagen to be by bike.
- 20 % more passengers to use public transport.
- Public transport to be carbon neutral.
- 20-30% of all light vehicles to run on new fuels such as electricity, hydrogen, biogas or bioethanol.
- 30-40 % of all heavy vehicles to run on new fuels.

Targets for City Administration

- Reduce energy consumption in municipal buildings by 40 %.
- Municipal buildings up to 2015 to meet the requirements of the 2015 classification and new buildings to meet the requirements of the 2 0 2 0 classification.

- City vehicles to run on electricity, hydrogen or biofuels.
- The energy consumption for street lighting to be halved.
- A total of 60,000 sq m solar panels on existing municipal buildings and new municipal buildings to be installed.

It may be noted that Denmark generates most of its electricity from wind. India generates most of its electricity by burning coal, and we have a tougher task ahead. Moreover the population of Denmark is low, a mere 5.6 million and decreasing! **Nevertheless let us consider if we can catch up with them and beat them to the goal of Carbon Neutrality by 2025.**

How Can This Be Achieved?

Lighting, Appliances and Water Heating

In the domestic sector most of the energy needs of lighting, appliances and water heating are met by electricity. If we implement all the measures suggested in the Domestic Consumption chapter, the demand for electricity in 2020 will greatly reduce. For that purpose we need to assume that all savings measures will be fully implemented. These measures are:

- All lighting is done by LED lights.
- Only five star rated appliances are used. This will reduce 35% of possible load due to appliances. DC appliances would reduce load further.
- 100% water heating to be done by solar water heaters. Solar water heater of appropriate capacity should be made compulsory for new as well as old buildings.
- All measures of green building listed in the 'Domestic Consumption' chapter will be religiously implemented.
- Savings due to behavioural change will be fully achieved.

The resulting scenario will be as follows:

Domestic Consumption	Million Units
Residential	
Lighting[ii]	439
Appliances[iii]	816
Water heating	0
Residential electricity requirement after behavioural savings	**1,255**
Commercial	
Lighting	300
Appliances	390
Water heating	0
Commercial (LT) electricity requirement after behavioural savings	**690**
Total Domestic Electricity Requirement	**1,945**

Thus, total domestic electricity requirement would be 1,945 MU.

Cooking

Generally, petroleum fuel, mainly LPG, is used for cooking. Can we do all cooking on electricity? Yes, we can. Induction cookers and microwave ovens can be used for cooking and for re-heating of food and liquids. They are more efficient than gas stoves. The heating efficiency of an induction cooker is 80% whereas that of an LPG stove is 40%[iv]. This is because only a fraction of the heat content of the LPG flame is used for heating the container and the food, majority being lost to the atmosphere. There is no such heat loss to the atmosphere in case of an induction cooker. Microwave ovens are even more efficient since the entire electrical energy is used to heat the food, none is wasted in heating the container.

To replace 1 kg LPG we require about 6.57 units of electricity[v]. If everyone shifts to electric cooking devices, we will need 1,583 million units of electricity for cooking.

LPG used in one year (kilotonnes)	241
Conversion factor (kilotonnes of LPG to million units)	6.57
Electricity required if electric cooking is used (million units)	**1,583**

Transport

Generally, vehicles use petroleum fuel. Can all these vehicles run on electricity? Yes, they can. Scooters, motorcycles, cars and buses can all run on batteries. These batteries can be charged at night and the stored energy be converted to motion through electric motors. Electric vehicles are efficient. Their overall efficiency is 70% (efficiency of conversion of electric energy into mechanical energy) whereas petroleum fuel based systems are relatively inefficient. Their overall efficiency, considering the Indian traffic conditions, is only 20%. Considering the calorific value of petroleum fuel and overall efficiencies, we will need 760 million units of electricity every year for running electric vehicles.

Year 2020	Petrol	Diesel	CNG	Total
Annual Fuel Consumption (Kilotonnes)	97	97	22	
Conversion factor[vi] (kWHr/kg fuel)	3.55	3.41	3.81	
Electricity required (million units)	**344**	**332**	**84**	**760**

If we implement all the measures suggested in the Domestic Consumption and Transport chapter and that too 100%, the demand for electricity in 2020 will be reduced to the levels shown in the table below.

	Million Units per year
Domestic Electricity	1,945
Cooking Electricity	1,583
Transport Electricity	760
Total Electricity required	**4,288**

Can we generate 4,288 million units of electricity by solar panels in Pune itself? That would be clean energy, free of any CO_2. Again, the answer is 'Yes'. We can generate 4,288 million units of electricity through solar panels mounted on our rooftops.

One rooftop can support 60 sq m of solar panels and can generate 73 units of electricity per day. There are 183,369 non-slum residential rooftops in Pune which can generate 4,871 million units of carbon free electricity per day! Sounds incredible? We present detailed calculations below:

Pune's Solar Potential

260 Watt panels with an area of 1.4 m^2 to 1.6 m^2 are currently available. This means solar panels have an energy conversion factor of about 162 Watts/$m^{2\,vii}$. The energy conversion efficiency of solar panels is predicted to increase by 50% by 2020. This increased efficiency will lead to power output of 243 Watts/m^2.

No. of households[viii]	916,846
Slums (40%)	366,738
Non-slums (60%)	550,108
No. of buildings considering 3 floors each	183,369
Rooftop solar panels per building (m^2)	60
Watts per sq.m	243
Plant Load Factor	20.8%
Total units produced per day	73
Units from one rooftop solar panel per year	26,566
Million units produced in Pune per year	**4,871**

In other words, we can satisfy the entire energy demand of the domestic and transport sector by solar RTPV installation.

111

Economics of Solar Rooftop Installations

It is a generally accepted notion that solar RTPV are not economically viable. Let us study that issue in greater detail. Four scenarios need to be considered: the present scenario, and the effect of subsidy, cost reduction, and increase in conversion efficiency. Presently solar entrepreneurs are quoting a price much higher than ₹ 80,000/kW. However standardisation, mass production, automation and bulk buying would bring down the cost to ₹ 80,000/kW. After all, there is a market for installing 183,369 solar panels that will give a turnover of over ₹ 1,400 crore for Pune city alone. Surely, a large industrial house well versed in the art of mass production will come forward to bring the cost down.

	Present Scenario	Panel Cost down by 50%	Panel Cost down by 50%, efficiency up by 50%
Cost of Solar Panel (1 kW capacity)	44,000	22,000	22,000
Cost of Structure ₹	3,000	3,000	3,000
Inverter and Net-metering Cost ₹	20,000	20,000	20,000
Cabling Cost ₹	4,000	4,000	4,000
Total Material Cost ₹	71,000	49,000	49,000
Profit of Solar Entrepreneur ₹	9,000	9,000	9,000
Total Cost ₹	80,000	58,000	58,000
EMI (₹)^{xii} (A)	1,060	769	769
Annual Outgo (₹)	12,720	9,222	9,222
Units generated per day	5	5	7.5
Units generated per year	1,825	1,825	2,738
Cost per unit ₹	9	9	9
Annual income ₹ (B)	16,425	16,425	24,637
Annual Saving for first 10 years ₹ = (B)-(A)	3,705	7,203	15,415
Annual Saving after first 10 years (No EMI)	16,425	16,425	24,637

Required Policy Initiatives

- **Solar City Program:**
The Government of India has initiated a 'solar city' program. Currently Pune city is not included in that pilot program. So, in order to boost solar installations Pune will need to formulate its policy in line with the 'Solar city' program.

- **Technical Guidance:**
Installation of Solar RTPV panels is not a concern only of the State or Central government. Power generation as well as distribution companies are also stake holders. Technological support and infrastructural support should be given by MahaGenCO and MahaDiscCom (Mahavitaran) to such solar RTPV installations and feed generated power to grid . Since generation of 73 units per day would be far in excess of the requirements of the residents of a building, the excess has to be fed into the grid. MahaGenco and MahaDisCom should formulate policies that would support and encourage rooftop solar generation and feeding of excess power into the grid at ₹ 9 per unit. They should welcome this as they will not need to invest in solar power generation.

- **Linking RTPV to Property Transactions:**
Solar RTPV installation of $60\,m^2$ on a rooftop of a 3-storey building (or 10 sq m per storey) should be made compulsory for all new buildings. Building plans should be approved only if there is provision for Solar RTPV generation. This stipulation should also be insisted upon whenever any property transfer or renting takes place

- **Encouragement to Entrepreneurs :**

Entrepreneurs should be encouraged to instal solar RTPV and feed excess power into the grid. The residents would invest in batteries and inverters (most of them have already done so as a hedge against power failure). Entrepreneurs would arrange for the necessary connections of solar RTPV installation to the batteries and inverters that would feed excess electricity into the grid at ₹ 9 per unit. Government subsidy should continue till the panel cost comes down to 50% of the present level. It is predicted that this will take place by 2020.

- **Granting Loan Under Priority Sector Lending:**

There should be a bank dedicated to giving loans for solar RTPV installation. This bank should give loans at a concessional rate, say at 10%. Mahavitaran would first pay the bank's instalment and then pay the entrepreneur for the electricity fed by him into the grid. Since the investment would be safe and the payment would be guaranteed and timely, the bank would be happy to give such a loan at concessional rates. The bank should be financed by NABARD.

Neutralising Institutional Consumption

We still have to generate 2,289 million units to take care of institutional consumption. Fortunately institutional consumers are capable of generating their own electricity.

Institutional Consumption	Million Units Per Year
Total HT consumption 2010-11	2,069
Total Public works Consumption 2020	212
Public works LT 2020	8
Total	**2,289**

Institutional consumers should install wind mills of about 570 MW. Considering Plant Load Factor of 40%, 2289 million units can be generated by these windmills in one year. Investment required will be of the order of ₹ 40 billion but they will save ₹ 18 billion every year by not having to pay electricity charges. Of course, incentives by the Government by way of accelerated depreciation and maybe subsidy will be crucial.

Conclusion

By implementing the above measures, Pune can become the first carbon neutral city in the world. It will become a role model for other cities to emulate.

Appendix

[I]   http://denmark.dk/en/green-living/copenhagen/, Copenhagen Climate Adaptation Plan (http://subsite.kk.dk/sitecore/content/Subsites/CityOfCopenhagen/SubsiteFrontpage/Livingl nCopenhagen/ClimateAndEnvironment/~/media/9FC0B33FB4A6403F987A07D5332261A0 .ashx)

[II]   All lighting would be LED based. (It is considered that, currently all lighting is CFL which will get shifted to LED)

[III]   35% saving overall is possible. If we consider all non-star appliances will be shifted to 5 star. It is assumed that originally all appliances are non-star.

[IV]   Considering conventional LPG burner, higher efficiency burners are also available.

[V]

LPG to electricity conversion factor	
LPG Requirement (kg)	1
LPG Calorific value (kJ/kg)	47,300
Available energy in LPG (kJ/kg) **(A)**	47,300
LPG cooking efficiency **(B)**	40%
Actually energy used in cooking (kJ) = **(A)**x**(B)** = **(C)**	18,920
Induction cooker efficiency	80%
Electric energy required to give same amount of heat (kJ) **(D)**	23,650
Energy in 1 kWHr of electricity (kJ) **(E)**	3,600
Conversion factor (LPG to electricity) kWHr/ kg LPG = **(D)** / **(E)**	6.57

[VI]

Fuel to Electricity conversion factor	PETROL	DIESEL	CNG
Requirement (kg)	1.00	1.00	1.00
Calorific value (kJ)	44,700	43,000	48,000
Available Energy in fuel (MJ) **(A)**	44.70	43.00	48.00
Efficiency of engine	20%	20%	20%
Mechanical Energy at engine output (MJ)	8.94	8.60	9.60
Efficiency of electrical system	70%	70%	70%
Electrical energy required to give same amount on mechanical energy (MJ) **(B)**	12.77	12.29	13.71
Conversion factor Fuel to Electrical power (Unit per kg Fuel) = **(A)** / **(B)**	3.54	3.41	3.81

[VII]   Broachers of Jain solar, Vikram Solar,

[VIII]   Pune city sanitation plan (PMC website).

116

What is Biomass?

Biomass is the fourth largest source of energy worldwide and provides basic energy requirements for cooking and heating of rural households as well as for space heating and power generation.

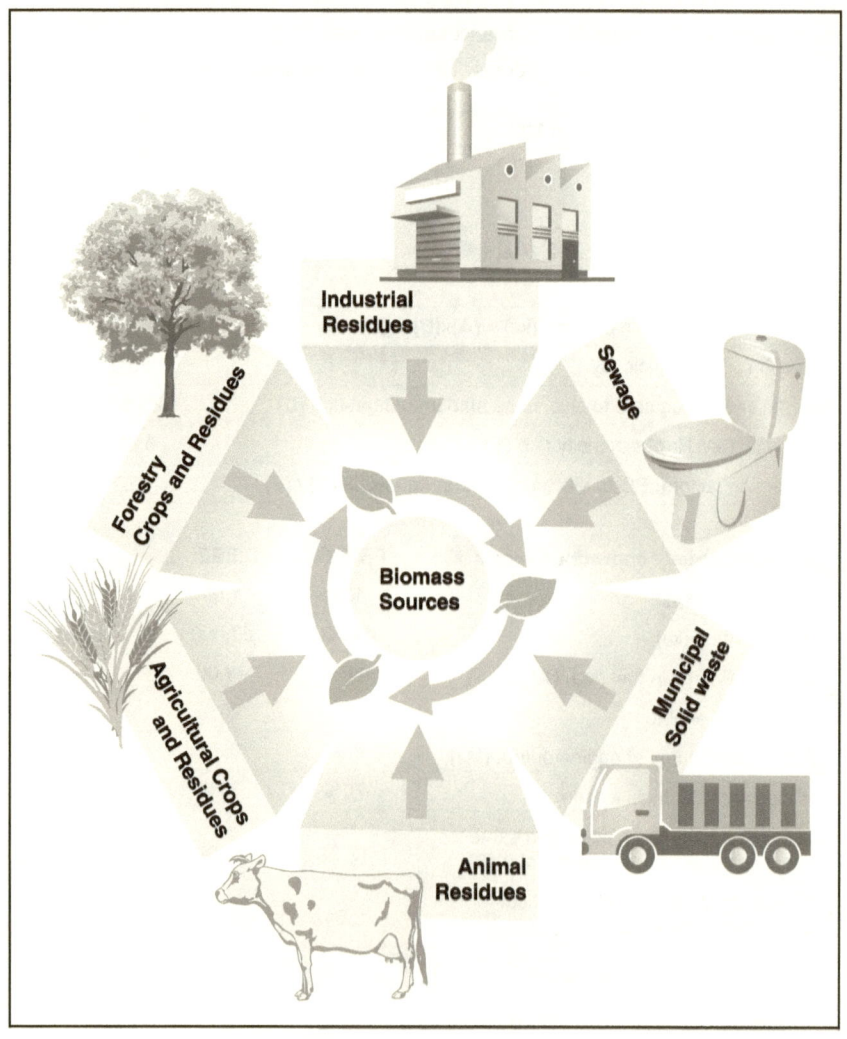

LET US AIM HIGHER
Carbon Neutral Pune
Using Biomass

In the earlier chapter we have seen how we can make Pune city carbon neutral. Suggestions included generating power by solar rooftop PV installations and windmills. In this chapter we will see if we can achieve carbon neutrality using biomass. Would you believe that biomass grown on about 12% of Pune district's area also has the potential to make Pune city carbon neutral?

Biomass can be combusted to generate power, to heat an oven or to cook food. This process is 'carbon neutral', because CO_2 emitted during combustion of biomass had already been absorbed when the plant was growing.

Agricultural Waste

Pune district generates approximately 26,000 kilotonnes of agricultural waste. If allowed to rot it would generate methane which is a potent greenhouse gas, but the good news is that it can be converted to energy. It has good calorific value. It can be compressed into briquettes that can be used as 'Green Coal' by power plants. These power plants can generate 26 billion kWhr of 'green' electricity per year, using the agri-waste.

Agri-waste can be used in two forms: briquettes and pellets.

	Briquettes	Pellets
Diameter	About 90 mm or more	About 10 mm
Compression	Loosely packed material	Densely packed material
	Low pressure compression	Compression done at higher pressure
Production cost	Comparatively low	High production cost
Final cost	Cheaper (About ₹ 5 per kg)	Costly (About ₹ 15 per kg)
Use	Where needed in large quantity	Where needed in small quantity
Equipment	Volumetric requirement is high so equipment is bulky	Less volume required, so equipment is less bulky

Briquetting

Briquetting is a process by which shredded and dried biomass is compressed to the desired diameter using a hammer press. This can be used for combustion in boilers and furnaces to replace coal or furnace oil.

Advantages of Briquettes

- Safe and non inflammable. No risk of explosion.
- Any combustible organic waste can be used.
- Reduces problem of waste management.
- Earns additional income for farmer.

The benefits of use of agri-waste as energy resource are not limited to CO_2 neutralisation. It has great potential for rural employment generation. Money spent on fossil fuel for energy generation goes to foreign nations, but the money spent on agri-waste will be distributed in rural areas of Pune district. It will slow down rural- to- urban migration and reduce stress on urban resources.

Agri-waste is also used as food by farm animals; only the balance would be available for power generation.

119

Briquetting Plant

A briquetting plant of production capacity of 10 tonnes per day (double shift) costs about ₹ 3.5 million. (Smaller briquetting plants are available, so the cost of transporting agri-waste to the nearest briquetting plant could be minimised). Buying price for agri-waste would be ₹ 1 per kg while selling price would be about ₹5 per kg. Operational cost is about ₹1.5 per kg. Considering transport cost of about ₹1.5 per kg, profit could be about ₹1 per kg of briquettes. Thus the plant owner will earn ₹ 10,000 per day. Payback for such briquetting plant would be just about one year.

For electricity generation, an old plant of 1 MW can be retrofitted to consume biomass briquettes instead of coal. Investment required is about ₹ 10 million.

Payback period could be reduced by awarding fiscal incentives like accelerated depreciation benefits.

Napier Grass

Napier Grass is one of the most important forms of biomass. Due to its high photo-synthetic efficiency it produces more biomass per acre than any other crop. The hybrid variety of Napier (CO3) invented by Tamilnadu Agricultural University is recommended for plantation.

Napier Grass grows very fast. It has better calorific value than most other types of biomass. Dedicated Napier Grass plantations can guarantee a constant supply of biomass of confirmed quality.

> **Climate and soil** - Hybrid Napier Grass grows throughout the year in the tropics. The optimum temperature is about 31° C. Light showers alternated with bright sunshine are very congenial to the crop. Total water requirement of the grass is 800-1,000 mm. Phenomenal yields are obtained from fertile soil rich in organic matter.

Benefits to Farmer

The farmer would get a fixed and assured income through Napier Grass plantation. For a cash crop, the farmer gets about ₹ 50,000 per hectare per year (for dry land farming income decreases to ₹ 20,000 per hectare per year). If irrigated land is cultivated for Hybrid Napier Grass, the farmer will get more than this as shown below:

Production Constants		
Production (dry wt)	Tonnes / hectare per annum (Full irrigation)	35
	Income to farmer at ₹ 2,000 / Tonne	70,000

Biomass to Replace Furnace Oil

Biomass briquettes can be directly burned and can replace furnace oil in oil fired boilers. Considering its efficiency, 3 kgs of biomass briquettes can replace 1 litre of furnace oil. Cost of biomass briquettes is ₹ 5 per kg, while that of furnace oil is ₹ 40 per litre. Thus by using biomass instead of furnace oil, one can save about ₹ 25 per litre, since 3 kg of briquettes are required to replace 1 litre of furnace oil. Of course, some modification to the furnace would be required, costing about ₹ 350,000 (for a boiler consuming 333 litres of furnace oil per day or 1 tonne of briquettes per day). Thus payback would be merely 42 days as seen below :

Retrofitting cost (₹)	350,000
Consumption of Briquettes (kg/day)	1,000
FO replaced (litres/day)	333
Savings (₹/day)	8,333
Payback (days)	42

Biomass fired boilers are gaining popularity. Many industries around Pune have replaced their oil fired boilers with briquette fired ones. As of today briquette consumption in the Pune area is more than 500 tonnes per day and this is likely to increase exponentially.

Biomass to Replace Coal

CO_2 emission due to electricity generation is very high because most of the electricity in India is generated by combustion of coal. One unit of electricity creates 0.8 kg of CO_2. As we have discussed earlier, combustion of biomass is carbon neutral. So, there is a good case to shift from coal to biomass, which is carbon neutral.

We have already seen the economical viability of briquetting plants, consuming agri-waste as raw material. Biomass briquettes can be used as replacements for coal in thermal power plants. Considering thermal efficiency of 30%, one kg of biomass can generate 1.25 units of electricity.

We also envisage a shift from diesel/petrol to hybrid or electric vehicles. This will further increase electricity requirement. The source of such electricity should be cleaner and has to emit less CO_2 than petrol/diesel. Power plants using biomass briquettes fulfill that requirement.

---

1 kg of Napier Grass briquettes will generate approximately 1.25 units of electricity. (30% thermal efficiency). Total electricity requirement for electric vehicles is about 4 billion units per year (including domestic and transport demand) which will require about 300,000 acres (about 120,000 hectares) of land for growing Napier Grass. This electricity will have very low grid emission factor.

Biomass to Replace CNG

Biomass can also be used as feed for bio-methanation plants. From 1 tonne biomass about 300 kg biogas can be produced of which almost 120 kg will be methane. Methane has the highest calorific value and can be used in place of CNG. Methane can also be a good source of hydrogen which can be fed to fuel cells for generation of electricity.

Biomass to Replace LPG

As stated earlier, biomass pellets can be combusted into specially designed 'gasifier stoves'. These stoves are designed so that there will be no smoke and combustion will occur with blue flame. Blackening of utensils, which is the usual problem with biomass combustion, is eliminated.

Considering calorific value and combustion efficiency, 1 kg of LPG can be replaced by 3 kg of pellets. As 3 kg of pellets replaces 1 kg of LPG, it actually replaces ₹ 90 with ₹ 45 as energy cost. Energy cost is reduced to half.

Estimated 2020 LPG consumption	kilotonne per year	239
Biomass required for per kg LPG	kg	3
Total biomass requirement	kilotonne per year	716
Total land area required	Acres	51,210

Hybrid Napier Grass planted on 51,000 acres (about 20,400 hectares) would yield adequate amount of pellets to replace LPG requirement of Pune in 2020 !

Biomass Cookstove
To use pellets for cooking, a specially designed gasifier stove is needed, which will replace the traditional LPG burner. It costs around ₹ 20,000.

Continuous feed biomass cookstove
Combustion of biomass in the stove is a batch process. So, cooking has to be interrupted for filling the next batch of pellets. This can be solved with the help of a continuous feed biomass cookstove. This cookstove can be controlled as easily as a LPG burner, and cooking can be continued without interruption.

Municipal Wet Waste

Rochem (India) Pvt. Ltd. has put up a plant in Pune that generates about 6,500 units of electricity per day. It currently consumes less than half of the municipal solid waste (MSW) produced in Pune. Thus doubling of electricity generation is easily possible. That will generate about 13,000 units per day or 47 GWhr in a year. Pune's street lighting electricity consumption is less than that at 43 GWhr in a year. Thus we can meet street lighting demand through MSW! If PMC converts all lights to LED there could be some surplus electricity to run, say, pumps in public gardens.

Options available for MSW treatment and utilisation

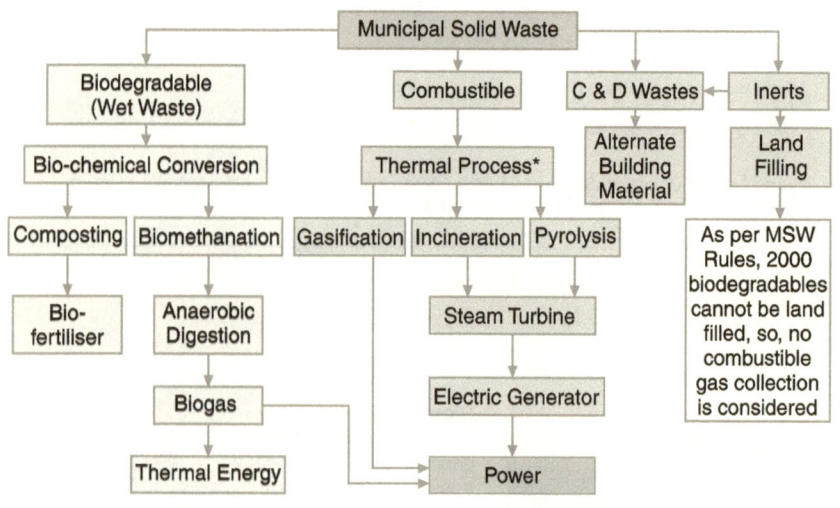

* RDF enhances the efficiency of thermal processes

Pelletisation Process

Municipal wet waste can also be a source of energy. Due to rapid urbanisation and increasing standard of living, wet waste is also increasing. This implies that, there is high potential for municipal wet waste to be converted to energy by pelletisation.

125

Wet Waste Disposal Process Flow Chart

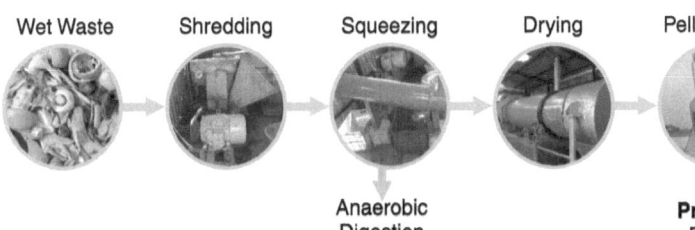

Wet Waste | Shredding | Squeezing | Drying | Pelletisation

Anaerobic Digestion

Product: Pellets

By-product : Biogas

By-product : Bio-Fertiliser

Comparative Analysis of Waste Processing Techniques

	Pelletisation	Incineration	Landfill
Emissions from plant	-	CO_2 and other	Methane. CO_2
Economic benefit	Yes, (₹ 12 / kg)	Yes, (₹ 5.8 per Unit)	-
By-products	Biogas, Bio-fertiliser	-	-
Sustainability	Most sustainable	Only after emission control	Wrong

Utilisation of Pellets

Pellets can be used in specially designed stoves as a replacement for LPG. The current market price of pellets is about ₹ 12 per kg. Using pellets will not only reduce CO_2 emissions but will also be economical. Economic analysis of pellet fired stoves is as follows.

Capital cost (10 kW stove) ₹	20,000
Pellets buying price (₹/kg)	12
Per day consumption (kg)	30
Cost of pellets (₹/day)	360
LPG replaced (kg/day)	10
Cost of LPG replaced (₹)	900
Saving per day (₹)	540
Pay back (days)	37

Pelletisation Plant Economics

Napier Grass is compressed to make pellets of about 10mm diameter. The volume of biomass decreases and they can be easily burnt in a compact and easy to operate gasifier stove as. Processing of biomass (shredding, drying and pelletisation) could be done by an entrepreneur. For 1 tonne per day plant, the capital investment is about ₹ 1 million and payback is only 405 days. This can be seen in the following table:

Pelletisation Press

Cost of raw material (₹ per tonne)	3,000
Operational cost (₹ per tonne)	6,000
Total cost of production (₹ per tonne)	9,000
Selling price of pellets (₹ / tonne)	12,000
Profit (₹ /tonne)	3,000
Total profit (₹ per year)	900,000
Capital cost (₹)	1,000,000
Payback (years)	1.11
Payback (days)	405

Benefits

India is blessed with fertile land, irrigation facilities, ample sunlight, regular rainfall and traditional knowledge. It is therefore natural that India should develop its economy based on agriculture. Agri-waste and Napier Grass have the potential to replace coal in power plants, replace furnace oil in food processing factories, replace LPG in cooking stoves of restaurants and replace CNG in bus transport. India will soon need more energy. Electricity is a clean energy, but is mostly generated by burning coal. Electricity generated by biomass is 100% clean since biomass has already absorbed CO_2.

127

There will be three beneficiaries: farmers who will benefit from the fixed income through rent or contract; entrepreneurs who set up processing plants will earn profits with a payback of around a year; and finally the buyers who will be able to buy biomass products such as pellets or briquettes at half the cost.

Issues
- Efforts are needed to develop continuous feed gasifiers with biomass combustion controlled by a single switch and appropriate flame control exactly like LPG.
- Delivery of biogas has to be user friendly, like LPG cylinders.
- Energy used and CO_2 generated in transporting Napier Grass to processing plant should be minimised. Plants should be located in a village or in a cluster of villages.
- Napier Grass should be harvested without disturbing the current land use scenario and cropping pattern.
- 'Biomass to diesel' technology is not yet foolproof and its throughput is not yet assured in the Indian context.
- Since production of biomass is an agriculture allied business, loans should be granted readily and cheaply as part of 'Priority Sector Lending' and at NABARD rates.

Conclusion

Biomass could play an important role to make Pune, carbon neutral. It can be easily converted to electricity and its cost is comparable with coal.

Appendix
[1] Planning Commission 'Report by task force on waste to energy'

Can We Make Earth a Paradise?

In the earlier chapters of the book we have seen that in the year 2020 we can reduce greenhouse gas emissions in Pune city to the levels of year 2010, that too while maintaining a rising standard of living. Steps needed to be taken by individuals and authorities to achieve this modest goal are also listed therein. All this is possible at zero net cost! since saving in energy usage more than offsets these costs.

Next, we aimed higher. Can we make Pune city 'carbon neutral' using existing technologies such as solar energy, wind energy and biomass? The answer, again, was 'Yes', and, once again, saving a tidy sum for ourselves.

If we extend the logic further, we can take say that it is possible to make every Indian city carbon neutral too. All of India can aim for carbon neutrality, since the rural areas have an abundance of biomass and consumption of electricity and petroleum fuel there is comparatively low. Abundantly endowed with renewable sources of energy such as solar, wind, hydroelectric and biomass, India as a whole can be carbon neutral too.

The Government of India has estimated that 749 Gigawatts of green energy can be generated if only 3% of wasteland is used for solar PV electricity generation. Why should we use only 3% of wasteland for this purpose? If we use 50% of wasteland for this purpose, we can generate

12,500 Gigawatts of green energy that will enable us to reach Japan's standard of living! Gujarat has even used the space over water canals for this purpose. So using 50% of wasteland for this purpose does not seem to beyond the realm of possibility. Investment should be financed from carbon tax.

Potential of generating green energy from other sources like hydroelectric, wind energy, biomass, tidal energy and wave energy is equally large especially if we add the potential of hydroelectric power in Nepal and Bhutan, so, making India carbon neutral, the ultimate in sustainability, is feasible and possible. Not just that, we should positively strive for it. It will eliminate our dependence on oil from the Middle East. Not only will we save foreign exchange and stop wealth transfer to these nations, it would also be strategically important for us. U.S.A. has made itself energy independent over the last few years, and that has altered the strategic scenario of the world. India, too, should use her ample natural resources and make herself energy independent and improve her security. If a thickly populated nation like India can do it, the entire world can too. India has 17.5% of the world's population but only 4.3% of water and 1.9% of landmass.

Making the world carbon neutral would usher in a veritable paradise on earth. Once again. This is one important step the human race must take.

New Technologies for Green Growth

Earlier in this book we have seen many ways to curb CO_2 emissions. Let us now consider some innovative techniques which will help us to further reduce CO_2 emissions while achieving a higher standard of living.

Micro Hydro

Some of us have seen a demonstration of micro-hydro technology in the movie 'Swades'. Where small dam is built near a village and electricity is generated. Large hydro power plants require heavy investment and their gestation period is high. Micro hydro power plants require much less investment.

Micro hydro is cheaper since it can be built by community participation. It is also helpful for watershed management and soil conservation.

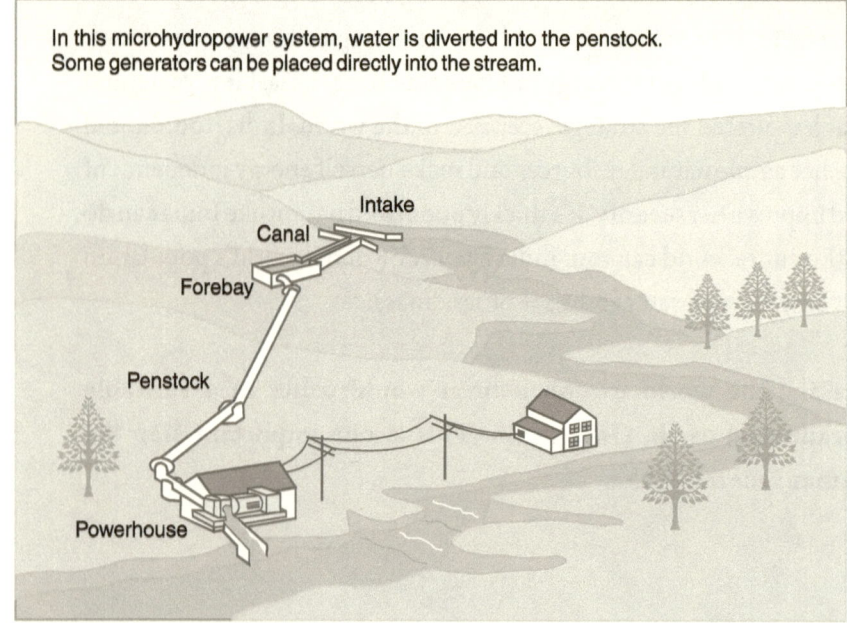

In this microhydropower system, water is diverted into the penstock. Some generators can be placed directly into the stream.

Micro hydro typically produces up to 100 kW of electricity using the natural flow of water. These installations can provide power to an isolated small community, or are sometimes connected to electric power networks. There are many such installations around the world, particularly in developing nations as they can provide an economical source of energy without having to incur the cost of purchasing fuel.

> **Ministry of New and Renewable Energy has availed scheme for development and installation of small hydro power plants (Upto 100kW capacity). About ₹ 400 can be availed per kW installation.**

Light Pipe

There are many buildings with areas where natural light cannot reach and artificial lights are required to be 'on' for the whole day. This problem can be solved by installation of a 'light pipe'.

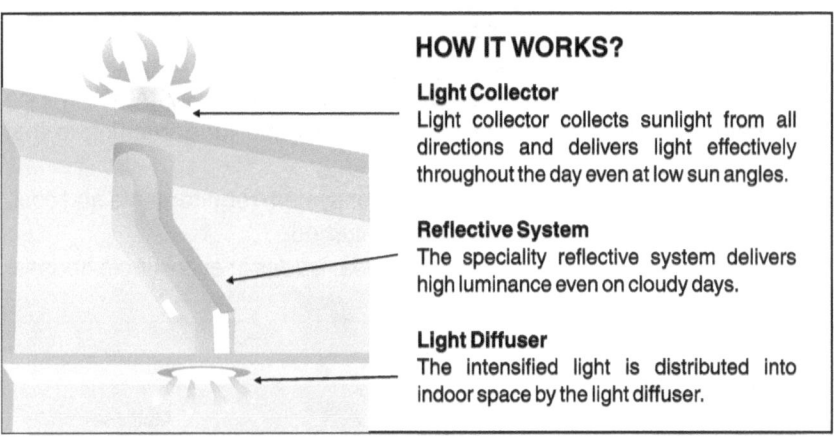

HOW IT WORKS?

Light Collector
Light collector collects sunlight from all directions and delivers light effectively throughout the day even at low sun angles.

Reflective System
The speciality reflective system delivers high luminance even on cloudy days.

Light Diffuser
The intensified light is distributed into indoor space by the light diffuser.

Carbon Sequestration

One tree absorbs around 21 kg of CO_2 per year. About 3,000 trees could be planted on one acre land. Thus 63 tonnes CO_2 will be absorbed by 1 acre of plantation.

Algae to Biofuel

Algae are simple microscopic organisms that live in water and grow hydroponically. They do not need soil and land, and do not compete for scarce fresh water resources. Algae function just like plants. Under plenty of sunlight, these organisms grow by photosynthesis, absorbing carbon dioxide (CO_2) and organic nutrients present in the water. They can double their mass several times a day! Depending on the species, up to half their mass is made up of lipids – natural oils. These oils can be extracted and used as straight algal 'crude', or refined to higher-grade hydrocarbon products ranging from biodiesel to biojet fuel for aircraft. Strains of algae that produce more carbohydrate than oil can be fermented to make bioethanol and biobutanol. Algae biofuels contain no sulphur, are non-toxic and are biodegradable. A number of strains produce fuel with energy densities comparable to those of conventional fossil fuels.

Sewage to Energy

Ideally sewage should be treated at source to eliminate its transportation and reduce its energy and volume requirement in Sewage Treatment Plants.
- Water from sewage would be treated immediately and thus it will be possible to recycle and reuse this treated water for gardening in that campus itself.
- This reduction in volume reduces further system requirements and cost, thus leading to reduction in energy consumed.
- This technology can be used for societies, *wadas* or even single houses.

Biodigester Toilets Designed By DRDO

The toilet has a tank fitted below the commode. The tank has sheets with bacteria embedded. When waste comes in contact with bacteria it gets converted to water and methane. Produced methane can be used as source of energy.

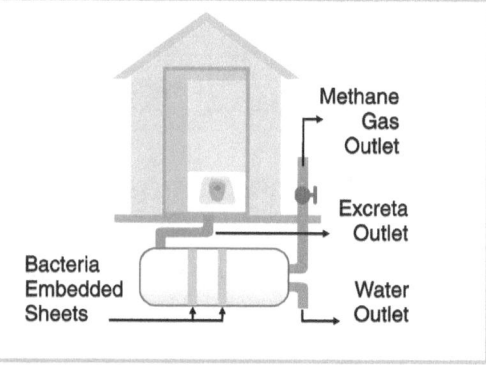

Modification For Railways A special lid allows for non-biodegradables like plastic bottles to be flushed out. The excreta enters through a separate opening into the digester tank.	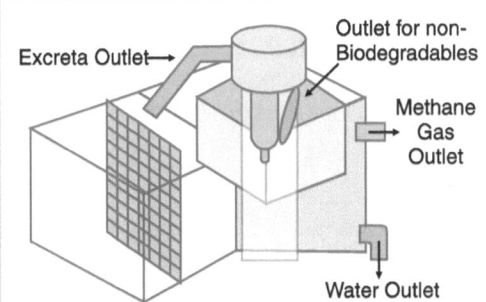
Modification For Areas With High Water Table The tank has several chambers. This increases the retention time of the waste and provides more surface area to break down the waste.	

Road to Rail Transport

Cities across the globe are shifting from road transport to rail transport. It is a shift from frictional movement to rolling movement, and it leads to lower frictional losses and higher efficiency.

Advantages Of Intra-City Rail Transport

- Cost effectiveness: Cost per person per kilometre is almost half that of with a diesel bus.
- Energy Saving: Trams require only 30% energy as that of bus/ road transport.
- Reduce CO_2 emissions: Trams run on electricity which can be generated from renewable energy sources, which will be emission free.
- Other environmental bonus: Trams are 'silent' as compared to diesel buses. Replacing the engine with an electric motor eliminates vibrations and sound.
- Due to absence of rubber tyres and complex engine, puncture and breakdown problems are reduced, making trams more reliable.
- After retiring from service trams can be recycled up to 90%.

Specific energy consumption per passenger kilometre for various modes of transport is given. It is evident that rail has the least specific energy consumption.(source: Planning commission's report on 'low carbon strategies for inclusive growth' chapter transport , pg69)

Specific Energy Consumption	Thousand Joules Per Passenger km
Cars & Jeeps	803
Two Wheelers	398
Taxis	1,338
Three Wheelers	619
Bus	196
Omno-bus	502
Rail	71
Air	1,266

TRAM	
95.488	kW
1	hr
95.488	kWhr
30	speed (kmph)
3.182933	units per km
70	ridership
0.04547	units per p-km
0.8	emission factor
0.036376	CO_2/ p-km

Feasibility
Pune city already has dedicated tracks meant for BRT. These tracks are well defined and fenced and can be used for trams. Only capital cost required is cost incurred for rails and overhead wires.

Induction Cars

'Induction car' is an innovative technology in which a car gets charged while driving. Electric coils buried under the road are connected to power inverters. These coils transfer power, by induction, to a 'pick up' system installed in the car, which charges batteries and drives the motor. This technology reduces the need for batteries to $1/5^{th}$. Use of OLEV (Online Electric Vehicles) is very beneficial for fixed route public transport.

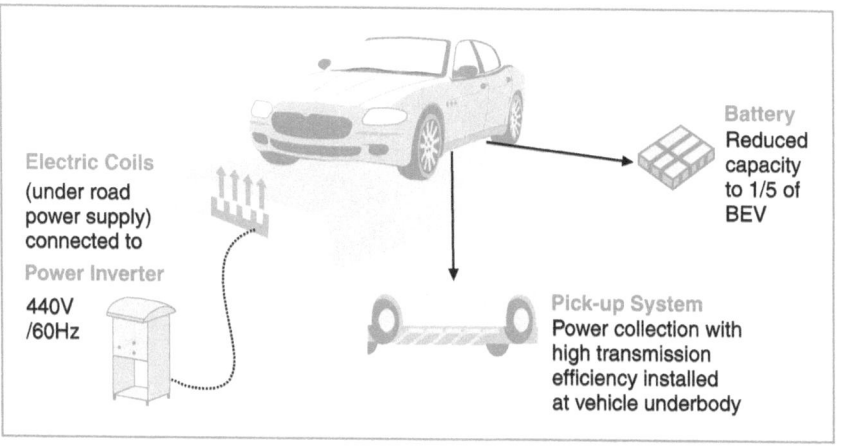

Battery Reduced capacity to 1/5 of BEV

Electric Coils (under road power supply) connected to **Power Inverter** 440V /60Hz

Pick-up System Power collection with high transmission efficiency installed at vehicle underbody

WaterTransport

Pune is blessed with four rivers that cut the city diagonally. The Mula flows parallel to Sinhagad Road while the Mutha connects Khadki and PCMC to Pune city. The Mula-Mutha can be used as waterways to link Pune suburbs to Pune city. Intracity water transport is not a new concept. In many metro cities across the globe water transport is regarded as an important mode of public transport.

Advantages of water transport
- Reduced energy consumption: Buoyancy of water helps the boat to float and friction between water and boat surface is lesser than between road and tyres of a vehicle.
- Saving of time: Since there would be no traffic congestion travel time can be saved .
- Use of water transport will add to the tourism potential of Pune city.
- Constant level of water will be required to enable water transport. This will also help to maintain the river ecosystem .

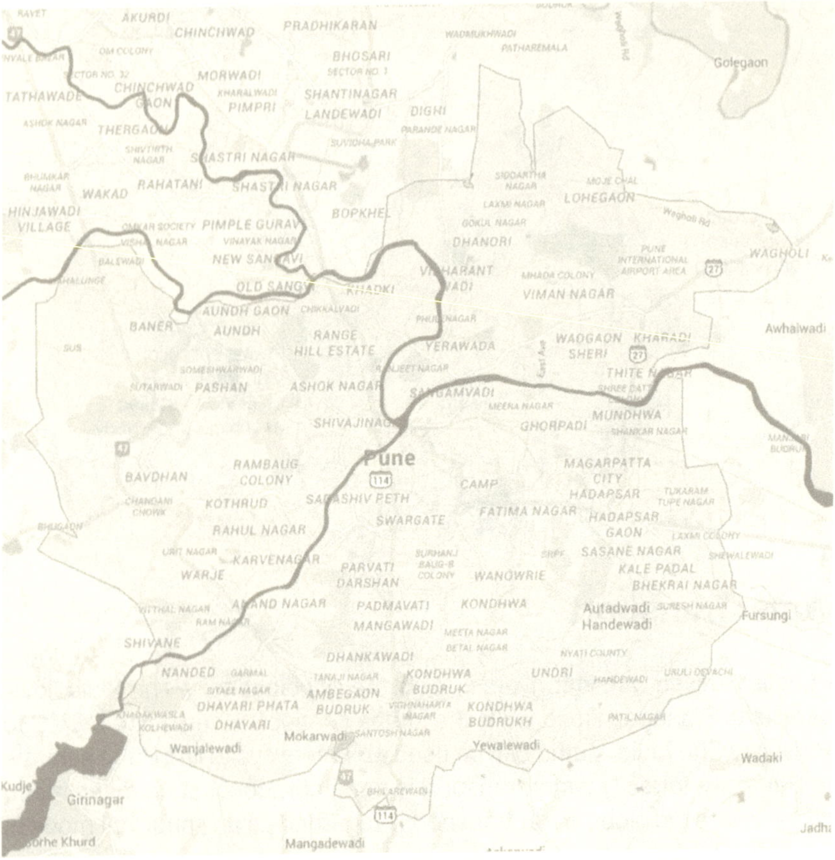
AKURDI
CHINCHWAD
PRADHIKARAN
BHOSARI
MORWADI
TATHAWADE
CHINCHWAD GAON
PIMPRI
SHANTINAGAR
LANDEWADI
DIGHI
THERGAON
SHASTRI NAGAR
WAKAD
RAHATANI
HINJAWADI VILLAGE
PIMPLE GURAV
NEW SANGAVI
OLD SANGVI
BOPKHEL
DHANORI
LOHEGAON
WAGHOLI
Golegaon
VIMAN NAGAR
AUNDH GAON
AUNDH
BANER
RANGE HILL ESTATE
YERAWADA
WADGAON SHERI
KHARADI
PASHAN
ASHOK NAGAR
SANGAMVADI
THITE NAGAR
MUNDHWA
SHIVAJINAGAR
GHORPADI
Awhalwadi
Pune
BAVDHAN
RAMBAUG COLONY
KOTHRUD
SADASHIV PETH
CAMP
MAGARPATTA CITY
HADAPSAR
SWARGATE
FATIMA NAGAR
HADAPSAR GAON
RAHUL NAGAR
SASANE NAGAR
KARVENAGAR
WARJE
PARVATI DARSHAN
WANOWRIE
KALE PADAL
BHEKRAI NAGAR
ANAND NAGAR
PADMAVATI
KONDHWA
Autadwadi Handewadi
Fursungi
MANGAWADI
SHIVANE
DHANKAWADI
NANDED
KONDHWA BUDRUK
UNDRI
AMBEGAON BUDRUK
DHAYARI PHATA
DHAYARI
KONDHWA BUDRUKH
Wanjalewadi
Mokarwadi
Yewalewadi
Wadaki
Kudje
Girinagar
Mangadewadi

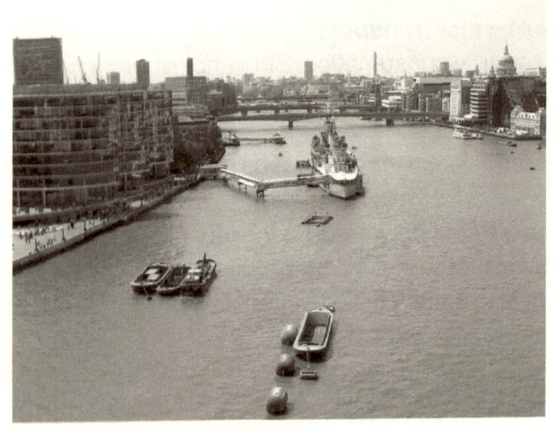

Tidal Energy

India has a long coastline where tides are strong enough to move turbines for electrical power generation. The Gulf of Cambay and the Gulf of Kutch in Gujarat on the west coast have a high tidal range of 11m and 8m with average tidal range of 6.77m and 5.23m respectively.

In case of the Ganges Delta in the Sundarbans the high tidal range is 5m, with an average tidal range of 2.97m. The estimated power potential is of the order of 8000 MW with about 7000 MW in the Gulf of Cambay and about 1200 MW in the Gulf of Kutch in Gujarat and about 100 MW in the Sunderbans region.

The MNRE has sanctioned a project for setting up a 3.75 MW demonstration tidal power plant at Durgaduani Creek in Sunderbans, to the West Bengal Renewable Energy Development Agency (WBREDA), Kolkata. The National Hydro Power Corporation Ltd. (NHPC) is executing the project on a turnkey basis

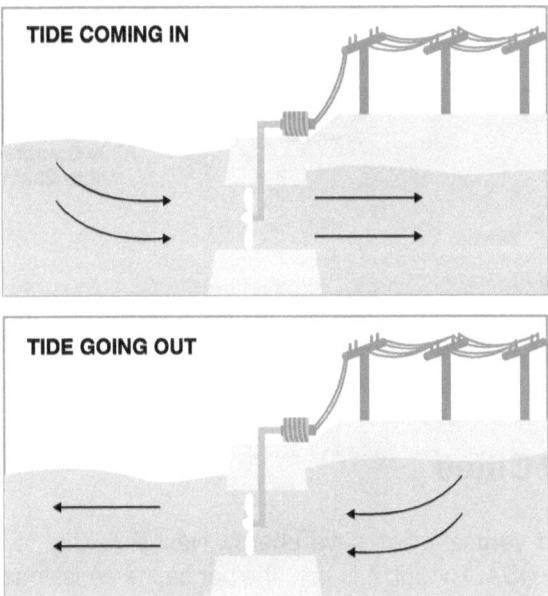

This tidal electricity generation works as the tide comes in and again when it goes out. The turbines are driven by the power of the sea in both directions.

Wave energy

Wave energy transfers energy from waves to usable electricity. Since 1890 attempts have been made to harness power from wave energy.

The sun causes a temperature difference between land and sea. This temperature difference results in the formation of wind. Wind at the sea shore pushes water to form waves.

Wave energy can be harnessed in many ways; oscillating water column (OWC) is the most popular one.

In OWC technology, a room called the 'Capture Chamber' is built on the sea shore. Oscillation of water compresses air and the air is pushed out of the room. When the wave is lower, it creates a vacuum, which sucks air in . This air movement rotates the turbine and an alternator coupled to it, which generates electricity.

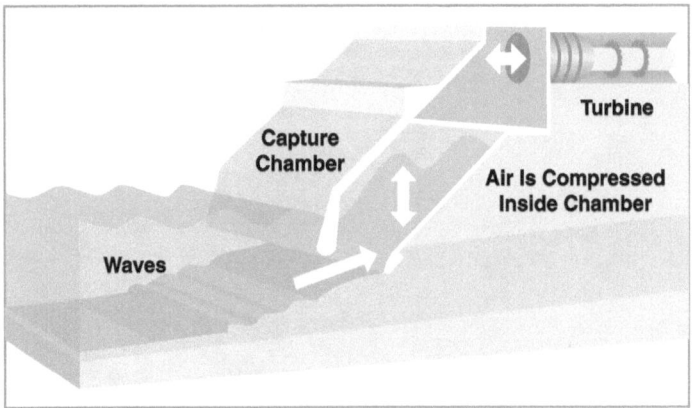

Compact Cities

Compact and vertical cities save energy. New York City is probably the richest city in USA. Though it is rich, the per capita emissions of New York are lowest among American cities.

This is due to the compactness of its city structure. In addition NYC has an efficient and well managed underground metro network. This has reduced emissions due to transport to a large extent. NYC has proved that compact cities minimise CO_2 emissions.

Per Capita GHG Emissions for Cities

Country / City	GHG Emissions (tonne CO_2 eq/capita)	Country / City	GHG Emissions (tonne CO_2 eq/capita)
USA	23.59	Los Angeles	13.0
Austin	16.2	Menlo park	16.37
Baltimore	14.4	Miami	11.9
Boston	13.3	Minneapolis	19.8
Chicago	12.0	New York City	7.9
Dallas	15.2	Portland, OR	13.5
Denver	21.5	San Diego	11.4
Houston	14.1	San Francisco	10.1
Philadelphia	11.1	Seattle	14.8
Juneau	14.37	Washington, DC	19.70

Source: siteresources.worldbank.org

Holographic Conferencing

Travelling for a conference? Old idea. Imagine instead if you could attend the conference without moving out of your home. This will save energy (and emissions). Holographic conferencing is a concept where conferences are conducted through 3D images of participants. There is no need for participants to be actually present at one venue. 3D conferences will obviously save travel by the participants. In the globalised scenario this facility would be a great boon to MNCs. It would save energy too .

Solar Concentrators /Towers

The solar power tower (known as 'central tower' power plants or 'heliostat' power plants or power towers) is a type of solar furnace using a tower to receive focussed sunlight. It uses an array of flat, movable mirrors (called heliostats) to focus the sun's rays upon a collector tower (the target).

A concentrated solar thermal plant is also a viable solution for renewable, pollution-free energy. Early designs used these focussed rays to heat water, and used the resulting steam to power a turbine. Newer designs using liquid sodium have been demonstrated, and systems using molten salts (40% potassium nitrate, 60% sodium nitrate) as the working fluids are now in operation. These working fluids have high heat capacity, which allows power to be generated even when the sun is not shining.

Fuel Cell Technology

In a fuel cell, electricity is produced by combining hydrogen and oxygen. Ion exchange between hydrogen and oxygen generates electricity. Hydrogen can be obtained from methane (biogas) generated from either MSW or Napier Grass. This electricity can be pumped to grid or used locally. Fuel cells can be charged at 'hydrogen' pumps. They are compact and so can be easily carried.

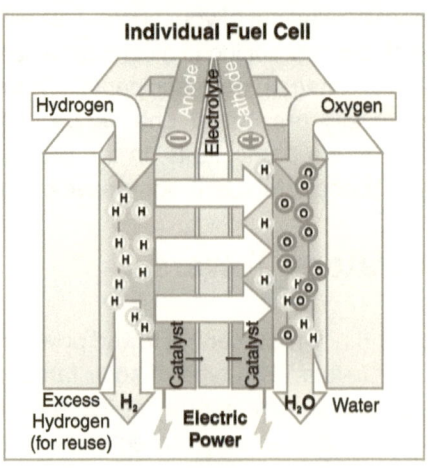

Nanotechnology

Nanotechnology is engineering at 'nano' scale. When 1 millimetre is divided into one million parts, then each part is termed as 1 nanometre.

Advantages of nanotechnology

- Efficiency of solar rooftop PV and fuel cells will increase dramatically. This will lead to reduced prices and will be a giant leap towards sustainability.
- Non-staining apparel will not require washing; this will reduce water demand.
- Nanotechnology allows use of lighter materials. Energy required to move such lighter material would be less.

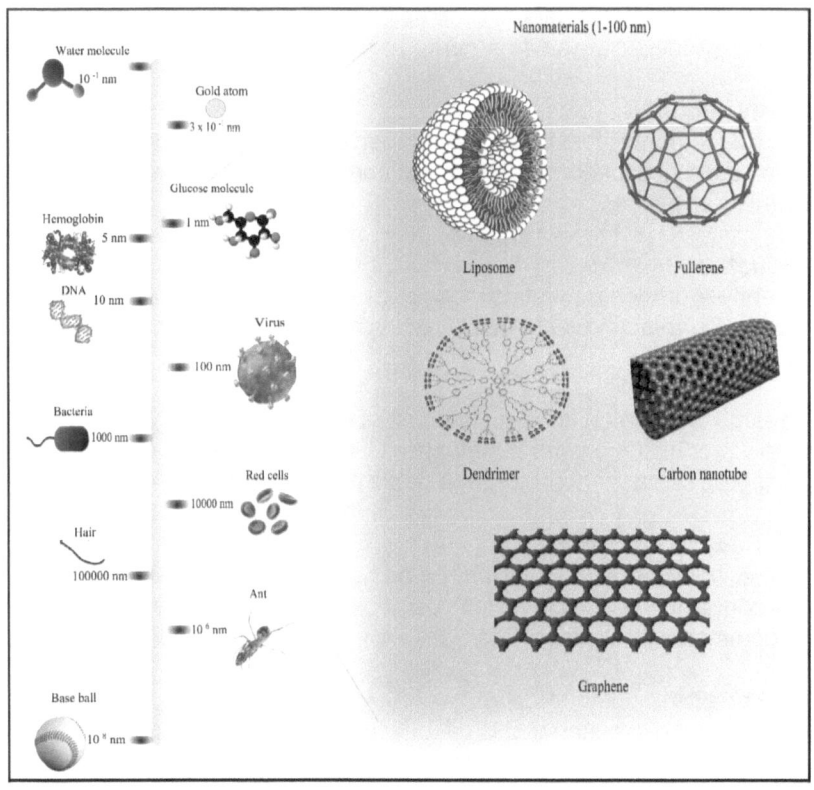

- Nano-filters would be of great help in water purification. These filters will allow only water molecules to pass. Water can thus be purified with much less energy. Pressure difference required can be provided by piston pumps coupled to cycles or even by swings.
- Nanotechnology can help devise material to capture CO_2.
- Safe hydrogen storage and other types of energy storage, can be solved using nanotechnology.

Hydrogen Economy

Hydrogen is the most promising future fuel.

Environment Friendly
When hydrogen is used as a fuel the only byproduct is water. Also, there are no environmental dangers like oil spills to worry about. No greenhouse gases are added to the environment.

Energy Security
The replacement of fossil fuel by hydrogen would eliminate dependence on foreign countries for energy. Hydrogen can be produced wherever we have electricity and water.

Production
Currently hydrogen is mostly produced by electrolysis of water, this method is costly. Or from petroleum gas, which is not eco-friendly since it produces CO_2.

Research is going on for reducing cost of electrolysis and for environment friendly production e.g. from methane (CH_4), which can be easily obtained by anaerobic treatment of bio-degradable waste (biogas).

High Cost at User Point
Fuel cell vehicles (FCVs), which run on hydrogen, are currently expensive than conventional vehicles. However, costs have decreased significantly and commercially available FCVs are expected in next few years.

Fuel Storage
Being the lightest element, it is difficult to store enough hydrogen onboard an FCV to travel a distance comparable to that of a petrol vehicle. Some

FCVs have recently demonstrated ranges comparable to conventional vehicles.

United States of America has announced a 'Hydrogen Mission' which aims to make 'hydrogen economy' possible.

Energy from Space

Space-based solar power (SBSP) uses the concept of collecting solar power in space (using an 'SPS', that is, a 'solar-power satellite' or a 'satellite power system') for use on Earth. It has been in research since the early 1970s.

Part of the solar energy may get lost on its way through the atmosphere. To avoid these losses space-based solar power systems convert sunlight to microwaves.

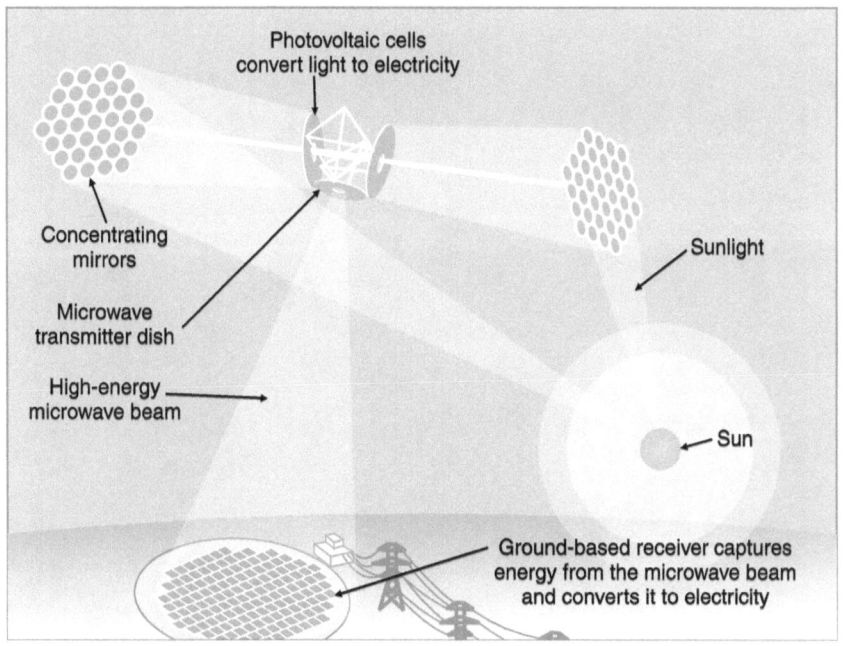

www.ingramcontent.com/pod-product-compliance
Lightning Source LLC
Chambersburg PA
CBHW031238260626
47169CB00007B/2354